Kylie [illegible] the face of a young girl pressed against the windowpane

The girl's hair was long and clung close to her head, as if she had just stepped from a shower. She waved.

Kylie lifted a hand and waved back, wondering what the girl was doing alone in the dark, drafty upper halls of the resort.

"Who are you waving at?" Michael asked.

"That girl, on the top floor." She pointed to the spot.

Michael glanced upward. "There's no one there, Kylie. You must have seen a shadow."

She looked up again, her eyes sweeping the length of the top floor. The windows were all empty, the small face pressed to the window moments ago, gone.

The hair on the back of her neck prickled and uneasiness rushed through her. Had she imagined the face?

"I could have sworn there was someone up there."

"Not possible. We keep the top two floors closed off during the winter months."

Kylie shivered. Perhaps returning to Cloudspin had been a mistake.

R

PRIMARY SUSPECT

SUSAN PETERSON

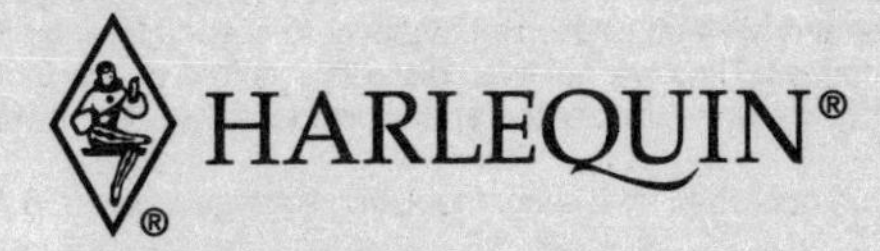

TORONTO • NEW YORK • LONDON
AMSTERDAM • PARIS • SYDNEY • HAMBURG
STOCKHOLM • ATHENS • TOKYO • MILAN • MADRID
PRAGUE • WARSAW • BUDAPEST • AUCKLAND

For Emmitt & Odin
May you find life as sweet and joyful
as you are to your loving parents.
Have a wonderful life, little guys.

A special thanks to Ann Drobnik for
taking the great pictures of the East Village.

ISBN 0-373-22894-5

PRIMARY SUSPECT

This edition published by arrangement with Harlequin Books S.A.

www.eHarlequin.com

Printed in U.S.A.

ABOUT THE AUTHOR

A devoted Star Trek fan, Susan Peterson wrote her first science-fiction novel at the age of thirteen. But unlike other Star Trek fan writers, in Susan's novel, she made sure that Mr. Spock fell in love. Unfortunately, what she didn't take into consideration was the fact that falling in love and pursuing a life of total logic didn't exactly go hand in hand. In any case, it was then that she realized that she was a hopeless romantic—a person who needed the happily ever after ending. But it wasn't until later in life, after pursuing careers in intensive-care nursing and school psychology that Susan finally found the time to pursue a career in writing. An ardent fan of psychological thrillers and suspense, Susan combined her love of romance and suspense into several manuscripts targeted to the Harlequin Intrigue line. Getting the go-ahead to write for this line was a dream come true for her.

Susan lives in a small town in northern New York with her son, Kevin, her nutball dog, Ozzie, Phoenix the cat and Lex the six-toed menace (a new kitten). Susan loves to hear from readers. E-mail her at SusanPetersonHI@aol.com or visit her Web site at www.susanpeterson.net.

Books by Susan Peterson

HARLEQUIN INTRIGUE

751—CONCEALED WEAPON
776—EMERGENCY CONTACT
798—MIDNIGHT ISLAND SANCTUARY
860—HARD EVIDENCE
894—PRIMARY SUSPECT

CAST OF CHARACTERS

Kylie McKee—All she wanted was to return to Cloudspin Lodge, pack her deceased father's belongings and leave. But something—or someone—is determined to see that she stays. Perhaps permanently.

Michael T. Emerson—The prime suspect in a string of bizarre murders, Michael retreats to his favorite vacation spot and childhood haunt, Cloudspin Lodge. But the murders seem destined to follow him there, making him question his own sanity and the possibility that he is the killer.

Detective John Denner—A seasoned New York City detective, he's determined to find the evidence to put Michael Emerson away for life.

Nikki Greenley—Cool, sophisticated and self-assured, Nikki isn't shy about going after what she wants, and she wants Michael Emerson. If that means following him up to the remote lodge buried in the mountains, then so be it.

Gracie Greenley—Shy, withdrawn and reeling from the effects of a difficult childhood filled with guilt and shame, Gracie reluctantly returns to Cloudspin Lodge with her sister, Nikki.

Craig Templer—Pompous manager of Cloudspin Lodge, he isn't happy with the invasion of unexpected guests during the lodge's off-season, especially since Michael Emerson ultimately has plans to fire him.

Andrea Greenley—Ghost child. The victim of a tragic accident eleven years ago, Andrea haunts the grounds of the old Adirondack lodge.

Steven Howe, Reggie Dumont, Heather Barlowe and Leslie McMasters—Nikki Greenley's faithful posse and fellow party revelers. They'll follow her wherever she goes...even if it's back to the place where all their lives changed.

Chapter One

Fog rolled in off the Hudson River, cloaking the darkened streets with a thick, choking mist of white. The limo turned onto Barrow Street and the tires hissed on the slick pavement.

Michael Emerson stared out the window, noting that the quaint buildings lining his street seemed to waver, appearing and disappearing within the grayish mist. It was an eerie effect, almost haunting.

He glanced away from the tinted windows and rested his head back against the soft leather seat. He tried to ignore the dull ache that pounded directly behind his eyes.

Heat poured through the vents, but the warmth seemed incapable of killing the chilling dampness that flooded the interior of the car.

Michael massaged his forehead with the tips of his fingers, a futile attempt to relieve the pressure. But the pain and pressure remained, the intensity increasing with each passing minute.

The headache had started during cocktails and continued on through dinner. The crush of the crowd and the overly loud music at the benefit dinner hadn't helped matters. At one point, he had excused himself from the head table and gone to the men's room. He hadn't wanted to take anything, willing himself to withstand the pressure. A punishment of sorts, a condemnation of his careless-ness. There was no getting around the feeling that the fall while rock climbing had been a stupid mistake.

Disgusted, he shook his head. World-class climber and he'd fallen on a simple rock face he'd climbed a million times before without incident. A disastrous climb that had resulted in the death of one of his good friends. Served him right that he suffered from headaches.

But recriminations were useless and he had realized that during dinner. In the end, he had relented, downing two painkillers his physician had given him after the accident, acutely aware that he had a speech to deliver.

Unfortunately the medication had produced no notice-able change, and he had ended up losing time while in the men's room.

Blank time. A yawning space of emptiness.

For how long, he wasn't sure. Twenty minutes? A half hour? An hour? All he remembered was standing over the sink in the cold stark bathroom, fighting a sucking, clawing pit of pain that had seemed determined to pull him under.

When he finally returned to the table, he was relieved that no one commented on his absence. Mainly due to the fact that they were all feeling pretty good, well into their third or fourth bottle of wine.

So, he had sat down and picked up where he'd left off, thinking to himself that it was as if time had stood still for a brief second.

"Looks like trouble up ahead, sir," his driver's voice broke over the intercom, interrupting Michael's thoughts.

He sat up and hit the switch lowering the tinted window between himself and Alex. Shifting forward, he peered out the windshield. Trouble indeed.

Halfway down the block, directly in front of his newly renovated town house, the harsh glow of police lights flashed in the thick fog. Several patrol cars, an ambulance and a black van were double-parked, and men in uniform flitted in and out of the thick shroud of fog blanketing the narrow street and sidewalk. Something was definitely up.

"Wonderful," Michael muttered under his breath.

"Want me to just cruise by, sir? Take you on out to the house in the Hamptons?"

For a brief moment, Michael actually considered telling Alex to do exactly that—cruise by, take the bridge and head out to his place on the island. Ignore the whole damn thing. But as soon as the thought flashed into his brain, Michael knew that wasn't the answer.

As weary as he was at the thought of suffering another go round with the NYPD, running was not the answer. He needed to deal with whatever waited for him a few feet away. Time to find out what had brought the police to his doorstep for a fourth time in less than six months.

The thought made the pain in his head shoot up another few notches.

"They know my license plate, Alex, and as enticing as your offer is, I'm going to have to talk to them sooner or later." He slid across the seat to the door. "Just pull up."

He reached for the door handle, prepared to climb out. Of late, he'd gotten pretty good at dealing with the police. They might not believe a word he said, but up to this point, he hadn't been arrested for anything.

A part of him wondered why no arrest. With all that had occurred over the past six months, even he was starting to have doubts about his innocence.

Alex slid the limo up next to one of the double-parked patrol cars and stopped. He started to get out to come around and open the door for him, but Michael laid a hand on his shoulder. "Take the car and go on home. I'll handle this."

Alex turned and leaned an arm on the shelf between the front and the back of the limo. "You sure you don't want me to come with you, sir?"

Michael shook his head. "No, I'll see you tomorrow morning, bright and early."

He grabbed the door handle and climbed out, cringing as his foot hit a partially frozen puddle. The thin ice broke and frigid water sloshed over the sides of his shoes and dampened the hem of his pants. Great. One more thing to cap off a lousy evening.

The fog parted, allowing Michael to see the front of his house. Yellow crime scene tape cordoned off the area and a tight circle of uniformed cops milled around. When they spotted him, they parted, allowing him access to the front of his home. There was no missing the veil of ill-concealed anger in their eyes.

As he stepped up onto the curb, Michael stopped short. The ringing in his ears and the ache between his eyes increased to the point of almost blinding him

A woman hung nailed to his front door, a ski pole jammed through the upper left side of her chest, a bright red stain spreading across the front of her skintight, white lace dress. Adrenaline hit Michael's bloodstream with a thundering rush.

Although her head hung forward, her luxurious chestnut-brown hair limp and her chin resting on her narrow chest, Michael had no difficulty recognizing her—Corinna Hamish, a former girlfriend.

There was no question that she was dead. The killer had shoved the pole up under her rib cage. The blood was dark and rich on the white lace.

In a daze, Michael moved closer. Anger ripped through his body, settling deep in the pit of his belly. How could this have happened again? How could another person he cared for been murdered and then left like a piece of discarded refuse on his doorstep?

He stared in disbelief, rage replacing confusion. This was the fourth victim in less than six months, and all the deaths were connected in some way to him. All the victims had been women he had known or dated. All women he'd cared about in some deeply personal way.

No wonder the police wouldn't leave him alone. It was as if the killer was leaving behind these grisly messages just for him. Messages he didn't understand or grasp no matter how hard he tried.

He stared at the metal spear stabbing her chest. He instinctively knew that the police would link the pole to him. Probably part of his skiing and climbing gear stored in the basement. As with the previous murders, the killer had set him up, implicated him in the crime.

He braced himself, preparing for the ordeal that he knew lay ahead. The three previous interrogations following the earlier murders had been grueling. The sight of Corinna's body told Michael that he'd soon be dealing with the same thing all over again.

"Getting to be quite a habit, isn't it, Emerson—" a deep edgy voice said from behind, "—you and I meeting over the murdered bodies of your ex-girlfriends."

Michael turned, not in the least surprised to find NYPD Detective John Denner standing behind him. His big hands were shoved into the pocket of his ill fitting pants, a scowl of suspicion and disgust crowding his craggy, disagreeable face. The man made no attempt to hide his hatred of Michael.

"Are you going to take her down or leave her hanging there?" Michael demanded, surprised at how easily the anger slipped into his voice.

He sucked damp air. This was not the time to lose his cool. Denner wanted that. Wanted him off balance and vulnerable.

"She deserves more than to be left hanging like that," he added in a softer voice.

Denner's gaze shifted to Corinna's body. "A few more pictures and they'll take her down." The detective smiled, but there was nothing warm or sympathetic in the stretch of his thin lips. "Mind telling me where you've been all evening?"

"I was at the Waldorf. A benefit dinner for St. Vincent's. Since I was their main speaker, I have plenty of witnesses to my whereabouts."

"I'll just bet you do."

Michael hated the fact that he had to account for his every move, but he also knew that Denner held firm to his belief that he was the prime suspect in all three—now four—murders.

"I can give you the names of several prominent people who can vouch for my whereabouts all evening," he said. "You're welcome to talk to all of them."

"Oh, you can count on me doing just that. In fact, I plan on checking and rechecking each and every name. And when I'm finished, I'll dig into where you've been every second for the last twenty-four hours."

"The only time I was out of anyone's sight was when I excused myself to go to the men's room." Michael shrugged. "For all I know someone might have seen me in there, too."

He didn't bother adding that he'd stayed in the men's room for more than a few minutes, trying unsuccessfully to deal with the headache.

His neurologist had told him that the troublesome headaches would last for a while. Mainly because a serious concussion can do that to a person.

But the pain from the headaches wasn't the only thing bothering Michael. Lately he'd become more concerned about the increasing blank periods, the blackouts.

But he didn't mention those to Denner. Something told him that admitting he'd lost time would put him in an even more tenuous position with the police detective. Better to try to deal with the blank periods on his own.

"Perhaps you were gone long enough to slip out the back door and finish off Ms. Hamish," Denner said.

"You'd like to believe that, wouldn't you? It would make your job easier."

"There's nothing easy about pinning you down, Emerson. But I'll find a way."

"I didn't kill Corinna."

Denner snorted. "You don't mind if we check that out for ourselves, right?"

Michael shrugged again, trying for a casualness he didn't feel. "Do whatever you need to do. Nothing I say has had much impact on your obsession that I'm the one who killed these women."

"Yeah, well, it's hard to believe a guy who is intimately connected to all the murder victims but keeps insisting he's as innocent as pure driven snow."

Off to the side, the crime scene photographer moved to a position directly across from Michael, snapping off pictures in rapid succession. The flash of the camera renewed the pounding in Michael's head. He glanced away, a part of him unable to comprehend the brutality of Corinna's death.

He reached up and rubbed his temple, trying desperately to clear his head. He needed his wits about him right now. This was not the time for headaches or the ugly sensation of fogginess that seemed to cloud his brain. The mist swirled around them, wet and clinging.

Although he'd been able to provide an iron-clad alibi for each of the murders, he knew it frustrated the hell out of Denner and the other members of the special task force assigned to the case. They wanted him to confess. Wanted the case closed with him behind bars for life or a needle in his arm.

"When was the last time you talked with Ms. Hamish?"

"Two weeks ago. We had lunch at Kristoff's."

"And that's when you gave her your typical kiss-off?"

"If you're asking if we discussed the direction our relationship was going, then yes."

"Not getting enough, huh, Emerson?"

Michael's hands tightened into fists at the crudeness of the remark. But he didn't bite. He'd gotten used to the detective's technique, familiar with Denner's tendency to try to push his buttons. No way did he plan on giving Denner the kind of ammunition he was fishing for.

"Corinna wanted more out of our relationship," he said. "She was a classy woman who always put things on the table. She was honest about her desire to see things between us go to the next level. I told her that as much as I liked her—enjoyed her company—I didn't see our relationship going any further."

"So you took her out and finished her off because she wasn't willing to accept your brush-off, right?"

"Actually we parted quite amicably. Corinna is—" he swallowed hard "—was a beautiful woman. She didn't want for male companionship. She knew how to move on. I have no illusions that she saw me as the only fish in the ocean."

Denner laughed, the sound harsh. Grating. He nodded in Corinna's direction. "You call a sharpened ski pole shoved through her chest amicable?"

Michael fingers tightened into fists, but again he kept his voice reasonable. "Of course not. But that doesn't prove I killed Corinna."

"Funny how every woman you've ever had a relationship with seems to be turning up dead. You don't find that unusual? Significant in some way?"

"As hard as this is for you to grasp, Denner, I'm telling you the truth. I didn't kill Corinna or any of the other women."

At least he was pretty sure he hadn't. God, please let me be innocent.

"Where have I heard that pitiful claim before?" Denner snapped his fingers. "Oh, yeah, that's right, four weeks ago, following the unfortunate demise of Ms. Karen Pearson—another of your former companions."

"You've already checked and rechecked my alibi for that night. You know there was no way I could have killed her."

"Not how I see things. I just haven't found out how you managed to slip out of your meeting without being missed." Denner smiled again, a barracuda eyeing his prey. "But rest assured, I haven't given up."

"No big surprise there."

Denner pulled out his notebook. "Give me the names of those prominent people who can vouch for your whereabouts this evening."

Michael rattled off a list of names and watched as Denner carefully recorded them. If he had any friends left after the completion of this investigation, it would be a miracle. Neighbors and friends were beginning to look at him with an unmistakable glint of uneasiness in their eyes. Not that he could blame them. He was beginning to suffer from his own doubts.

The crime scene photographer moved off, but still no one came to remove the pole and take Corinna down. Michael's stomach tightened into an unmanageable knot.

He couldn't stand seeing her hang there one more minute, her designer dress fluttering gently in the night breeze, revealing her slender white thighs in the harsh glare of the streetlights. Someone needed to cover her up. Give her the dignity she deserved.

Denner seemed oblivious to the stagnant stench of death hanging between them. He stood slightly hunched over, his hooded eyes seeming to bore gaping holes into Michael's. The man's suspicion and hatred was blatant, unmistakable.

Finally, unable to take it any longer, Michael ran up the steps. Before Denner or anyone else could stop him, he grabbed the pole and yanked it out. The end had been sharpened to a lethal point, explaining how it had pierced Corinna's slender frame with ease. He caught Corinna's body as she fell.

Denner rushed forward. "What the hell do you think you're doing?"

Michael ignored him as he gently laid Corinna's seemingly boneless body on the cold cement. He shrugged off his dinner jacket and laid it carefully over her face—a once classically beautiful face that had graced more than a few covers of high-end fashion magazines.

"It isn't right to leave her hanging like that," Michael said, squatting down to tuck the corner of his coat around Corinna's slender shoulders. "She deserves better."

"You should have thought about that before you nailed her to your front door. And quit messing with our crime scene or I'll have one of my guys run you in just on principle."

Michael sighed. There would be no convincing the police of his innocence. They had zeroed in on him like vultures on fresh meat. They'd work this angle until they found a way to pin the murders on him. Something told him their focus on him was so intense that there was a strong possibility they'd miss any clues to the killer's true identity.

He blinked, momentarily blinded by a flash of light. He glanced up to see several reporters gathering behind the crime scene tape. Another group of vultures had caught the scent and arrived right on cue.

No doubt they'd gotten a good picture of him leaning over Corinna's body. He knew that within a few hours photos of him would be splashed across the front page of all the local papers and on the early morning news.

He needed to think. To get away. Things were getting out of control. There had to be a reason for all these killings and he needed to figure out how he'd become the catalyst.

He straightened up and glanced at Denner. "Am I permitted inside?"

Denner paused and then nodded. "Sure. Just ignore the men dusting and tearing the place apart."

No surprises there. They'd done the same thing after each murder, attempting to find something, anything, that would firmly implicate him in the murders.

As he reached for the doorknob, Denner followed close on his heels. Obviously the man wasn't done with him yet.

His housekeeper, Hattie, met him at the door, her tiny hands clenched in front of her, an expression of concern cramping the lines of her bony face. "I'm sorry, sir. They have a warrant."

Michael patted one of her thin shoulders. This was the fourth time they'd searched his house. He was almost getting used to the indignity of the police invasions, but from Hattie's expression, he could tell she was more than a little unnerved.

"Everything is going to be fine," he reassured her. "You did the right thing letting them in."

"But they've torn everything apart again, sir." Her frightened birdlike gaze darted nervously toward the body behind him and then back. "It took us days last time to get things back to normal."

"Your boss should have thought of that before he went on his little murder spree," Denner said.

Hattie's face reddened, but before she spoke again, Michael guided her back into the front hall. "We'll worry about it later, Hattie. Just let the police do their job. Things will be back to normal eventually."

In spite of his reassurances, Michael wasn't sure *normal* was something he'd ever experience again. His life was a mess.

Hattie glanced at Denner and sniffed her disapproval. "They could at least have put things back where they belonged when they were done pawing through them."

"Not our job, ma'am," Denner said. "But then, I'm sure your boss has the money to hire extra help if he needs it."

Hattie gave another sniff of blatant disapproval and moved away, heading into the living room where a group of investigators were dusting every conceivable surface of her usually sparkling clean room.

Michael was sure she was watching the CSI staff's every move, suspicious that someone might pocket one of the expensive treasures tastefully scattered about the room. Treasures he'd obtained on his world travels, something he was fairly certain he wouldn't be doing again anytime soon. Not when he was the prime suspect in a series of four brutal murders.

"You have a loyal staff."

"Hattie's been with me a long time," Michael said.

"Long enough and loyal enough to lie for you perhaps?"

Michael didn't bother responding. He knew it was useless. Denner's mind was made up and nothing Michael said would change it

He headed for the marble staircase leading to the second floor and his bedroom. Denner didn't back off and followed him up.

"Quite a collection of artwork you have hanging on the

walls around here, Emerson. Aren't you worried about someone breaking in and ripping it off?"

"I have a good alarm system."

"Yes, you do. And that brings up an interesting point." Denner paused on the middle of the stairs, and Michael stopped, too, glancing back. Waiting.

"There's no sign of a break-in. Whoever entered the house with Ms. Hamish, fetched a ski pole and then nailed her to the front door. The killer had to have a key or someone let him in."

"How do you know they even entered the house? That is a common enough ski pole. Maybe the killer brought it with him."

"Possible. But there's one tiny detail that tells me that isn't the case." Denner looked down into the front hall, nodding at the Windsor chair standing in one corner of the front hall. "That's Ms. Hamish's coat lying across the back of that chair. Any thoughts on how it got there?"

Michael shook his head, his heart thudding hard in his chest. The coat put Corinna inside his house. The trap was closing tighter with each passing moment. "I have no idea. Did you question my staff?"

"Of course," Denner said. "No one seems to remember anyone stopping by."

Michael continued up the stairs, turning right at the top and entered the master bedroom. The technician dusting the window sill glanced up briefly and then returned to his work.

Michael surveyed the room, assessing the damage. It was a total disaster. Every dresser drawer was open, the contents dumped on the floor. All his clothes in his closet were pulled off their hangers and lay in a heap in front of his closet. The boxes on the shelf pulled down and emptied on top of the clothes.

Someone had tossed the mattress of his king-size bed to the side. All the pillows were split, the feathers spread across the sage carpet. It looked as though someone had slaughtered a truckload of geese. A few of the feathers still floated in the air.

Michael spied his suitcase sitting open in the corner of the room and the urge to get away hit him hard. He needed to get out of here and sort things out. Get his head on straight.

There was no way in hell he could stay in the house another night, another day. If he was somehow the catalyst in these murders, he needed to get as far away from the city as possible. Somewhere isolated. Quiet.

"I'm leaving town for a few days," he said, standing in front of the suitcase, his back to Denner.

"Like hell you are. In case you've forgotten, I'm conducting a murder investigation here. You're to stay put. I want to know where you are every minute of the day."

Michael turned around. "Are you charging me with murder?"

The beefy detective shuffled his feet, frustration flickering across his craggy features. "We'll go downtown for one of our little chats. Maybe we'll get lucky and you'll have a flash of conscience and admit to your guilt."

"Not likely. I'm not inclined to confess to something I didn't do." Michael swung his suitcase on top of the box spring. "But once you've checked out my alibi and found out I'm not lying about where I was all evening, I'm leaving town. I'm going to my house outside of Keene. You know the one. Your men have been up there to search it more than once."

"Yeah, I know the one, along with your three other homes outside the country, too."

"Don't forget the one outside of Park City," Michael added, unable to keep the sarcasm out of his voice.

"Not a chance." Denner laughed, the tone adding to the pain shooting through Michael's brain. "But then, you haven't been out to Utah in over a year. Of course, I had it checked out."

"Why am I not surprised?" Michael walked over to the clothes left in a heap on the floor and grabbed what he wanted. He stuffed them carelessly into the suitcase before glancing back at Denner. "I'll turn my passport over to the D.A.'s office in the morning. No passport, no chance that I'd leave the country, right?"

"I'm not a fool, Emerson. You have the financial means to leave the country with or without a passport."

"So, put a tail on me. Notify the State Police. Do whatever you need to do." He grabbed a few more items of clothing and threw them on top of the others. He zipped the suitcase shut and swung it off the bed, facing Denner head on. "But unless you're prepared to arrest me tonight, I'm leaving for Keene after our *little chat* downtown."

The look on the detective's face confirmed his frustration, but Michael knew there wasn't much Denner could do. "Ready? The sooner I answer your questions, the sooner I can leave town."

"You might want to put on a hat as I have no plans on sneaking you out the back door. No doubt the press is waiting to get more pictures of that famous face of yours."

"I'll be fine."

"Yeah, you're doing just fine, aren't you? Cool as a cucumber and too damn sure of yourself."

Resentment shot through Michael. The man didn't get it. He never would. "In case you've forgotten, all the victims of these murders meant something to me. I cared about each and every one of them."

Denner smirked, his disbelief obvious. "Yeah, right."

"No matter what you want to believe, their deaths, the way they died and the agony of their families has been first and foremost in my mind."

"Spare me, Emerson. I have more feeling for these women in my little finger than you do in your entire body." Denner rocked slightly on the balls of his feet, his hands clenching into fists. "Don't bother trying to make yourself out to be the victim. No one buys it, least of all me."

"That wasn't my objective. There's enough blame to go around, and that includes you and your elite task force."

Denner raised a questioning brow. "What's that supposed to mean?"

"I gave you a list of all the women I've ever dated. I've personally spoken with each and every one of them, warning all of them of the dangers. And yet, they're still getting picked off one by one. Why haven't you done more to protect them? Tell me that, Detective Denner."

Denner stepped in close, his expression tight with rage. He hadn't expected the attack. Didn't like being challenged.

But Michael didn't care. He knew he was right. The women deserved protection, and so far the police had failed miserably.

"Don't threaten me, Emerson." Denner leaned in, his

breath hot and smelling of onions and sliced deli meat. "We all know who is responsible for their murders. And once I get the goods on you, the killings *will* stop, and you *will* be sitting in my jail cell."

Michael didn't bother responding. There wasn't any reason to. Denner had proven more than once that he had a one-track mind, and that track ran in the direction of Michael being the killer.

He brushed past the man and headed for the door.

"Tell me, Emerson, why is it that I have the distinct feeling that more women you know are going to turn up dead with your signature all over them?"

Michael paused at the door and then turned slowly to face the cop. "I don't know, Detective, why *do* you feel that way?"

The sneer had twisted and transformed Denner's face into something ugly and unrelenting. "Because I can smell a liar a mile away. It's only a matter of time before I find the evidence to convict you. Time and patience. Lucky for me, you're running low on both."

Michael fought to keep the panic that surged up inside him off his face.

As much as he hated to admit it, he knew that Denner was right. He *was* running low on time and patience. And the killer, a man who didn't tire of advertising his message of death, seemed to have plenty of both.

With the headaches and blank periods getting worse, Michael had the distinct feeling he was closer to the killer than he wanted to admit to anyone—including himself.

Chapter Two

Two Days Later

Within a few minutes of turning onto the fifteen-mile access road leading to Cloudspin Lodge, Kylie McKee wondered if she had made a mistake. The road was worse than she remembered and the fact that she hadn't driven it in over eleven years didn't help.

Beneath a blanket of new snow, the pavement was pitted and fractured, and although Kylie was fairly certain the county plow had gone through earlier, pushing mounds of snow up onto the overflowing banks on either side, a new covering of snow had already started to pile up.

In the rearview mirror, she could see only the tire tracks from her car. Virgin snow in both directions. No one had passed in quite some time.

A quick glance at the dashboard told her it was already 4:15 p.m. Dusk was approaching with frightening speed, decreasing her visibility. In this part of the world, rural upstate New York, there were no street lamps to illuminate the way.

Dying light stretched out the shadows of the huge pines lining both sides of the road, and huge oaks, their branches whipped bare of leaves, reached to enclose the road in a spiny tunnel of darkness.

Kylie inched forward, trying to get a better grip on the steering wheel. She could barely see the road through the thick cloud of falling snow.

Reaching down, she fumbled for the button on the side of her seat, desperate to get closer to the windshield. No sooner did her hand leave the steering wheel than the back tires of her rented Honda Civic skidded on an icy patch.

She clamped her hand back on the wheel and eased her foot off the gas. Don't brake. Don't brake, she chanted, her voice echoing hollowly inside the tiny car.

The car went into a stomach churning slide across the middle line and headed for a ditch on the opposite side of the road. She tried steering into the skid. Pine trees whipped by the window in a blur.

"Damn!"

She fought the wheel and touched the brake in an attempt to ease out of the skid. The car straightened out, but not before the left front tire clipped the edge of the road, sending her bouncing along a deep rut for several hair raising seconds. Finally she was able to steer back onto the snow covered pavement.

Sucking in a shaky breath, Kylie guided the car back onto her side of the road. Lucky for her people rarely used the road during the winter, preferring to visit the lodge during the glorious summer months that were legendary in the Adirondack Mountains. If another car had rounded the curve during her skid, Kylie knew she and the Honda would have been toast.

A tiny trickle of sweat popped up beneath the collar of

her ski jacket and slid down the side of her neck. She didn't make any attempt to wipe it away. It was time to focus and keep both hands on the wheel.

Her shoulders cramped with tension as she realized she had made a big mistake. She should have listened to the clerk in the tiny convenience store in Keene who had warned her of the worsening of the storm. She should have waited until morning to make the trip to the lodge.

But she'd been too eager reach her destination, believing that the sooner she got there, the sooner she could leave. But now Kylie realized that she'd made a serious miscalculation.

Dark, heavy clouds rolled and tumbled overhead, pressing down on the tiny car and unloading a hail of snow and ice pellets with a vengeance. The sleet tinkled ominously against the windshield and froze into stubborn chunks beneath her wipers.

She reached out and pushed the defrost to high, savoring the blast of heat that poured out from the vents and flamed her cheeks. Hopefully the added warmth would melt the ice build-up and prevent her from having to stop, get out and chop at it with the pathetically small scraper sitting on the floor of the passenger's seat.

The precipitation covered over the icy patches in the road, leaving behind a deceiving blanket of slickness. The wheel shimmied harder beneath her tightly clenched fingers, making them ache.

Something told her that the standard all-weather tires on the little Honda weren't going to cut it. She should have rented a SUV. But as soon as the thought entered her head, she dismissed it.

Who was she kidding? She didn't have the cash to rent something as extravagant as an SUV. She'd barely had enough money to keep the economy car filled with gas for the eight-hour trip north. She was down to her last ten dollars and her bank account wasn't in any better shape.

She pressed the gas pedal, giving the car more speed, hoping the momentum would keep her on track. She needed to reach Cloudspin soon. The thought of ending up in a ditch in the bitter subzero January temperature outside sent a shiver of fear through her.

The sooner she reached the lodge, the sooner she'd find warmth. And the sooner she reached warmth, the sooner she'd be able to complete her business, hop back in the car and return home to her comfortable little apartment in the Bronx.

She smiled to herself without real amusement. Residing in the city had resulted in an increased hatred for the bitter, forbidding winters of the Adirondacks. She hadn't been back to Cloudspin in over eleven years.

Instead her father had taken on the responsibility of making the trips down to see her. But with him taking care of the lodge and her working on completing her fourth year of medical school, the visits had been few and far between.

Now he was gone and she was coming home to take care of business. Business that meant cleaning out the caretaker's cottage. A cottage she'd lived in throughout her childhood, witnessing at age eight the slow painful death of her mother from ovarian cancer and watching in wide-eyed wonder the wealthy patrons of Cloudspin vacation in their private, sprawling Adirondack paradise. The contrasts had been stark and painful, making her homecoming bittersweet.

She leaned forward and peered through the ice accumulating on the windshield. The comforting *thump thump thump* of the wiper blades soothed the tension in her shoulders. Getting closer.

Up ahead, she could make out the final S curve. A few miles beyond that and she'd reach the main gates of the lodge.

Relief washed over her as she eased the car into the final curve. But then, out of the dim light, something fast and dark flashed out into the center of the road.

A skier! Where in God's name had he come from?

Kylie hit the brake.

She gripped the wheel and watched in frozen horror as the car skidded toward the man poling to reach the cutaway trail on the opposite side of the road.

What kind of fool skied in a snowstorm at dusk? Not to mention doing so dressed in black!

Time shifted into slow motion and the car slid sideways, the tires silent on the smooth ice. The skier glanced up, his expression hard. Determined. He knew the danger.

He dug in, moving for the opening with quick, powerful strides. His shoulders bunched beneath the sleek black jacket and his muscular thighs strained to propel him out of her way.

"Oh, God, he's not going to make it," Kylie wailed.

But she was wrong. He reached the cutaway as she skidded past him sideways. She overcorrected and the car fishtailed.

A sharp crack filled the silence and she cringed. She knew without actually seeing it that one of her tires had hit the back end of his skis.

In the rearview mirror, she saw him stumble and then pitch forward into the snowbank.

She hung on and eased her foot onto the brake. The car slid to a stop on the opposite side of the road and the hood gently hit the snowbank.

Stunned, she sat perfectly still, unable to loosen her death grip on the wheel. But then squirts of adrenaline shot into her bloodstream, hitting her hard. She reached up and unsnapped her belt. As she reached for the door handle, she prayed she'd find him alive.

A blast of frigid air hit her, taking her breath away. She scrabbled for the back end of the car, and in her haste, almost tripped. Frantic, she grabbed for the side of the car and cringed as the cold metal stung her bare hands. She ignored the pain and the voice that warned her to go back for her mittens. She needed to check on the skier.

Across the road, the skier climbed to his feet and leaned over to brush the snow off his pants with brisk, efficient sweeps of his gloved hands. A sense of relief flooded her. He didn't look injured. He moved with the fluid motion of a natural athlete.

Kylie gingerly trekked across the slippery road, watching as the man bent down to examine the broken section of his ski. It had snapped directly behind the binding. He wouldn't be using that particular pair of skis anytime soon. She hoped she had enough money in her bank account to replace them.

He straightened up and a pair startling blue eyes, direct and unflinching, focused on her.

Kylie's heart sank. There was no missing the smear of blood seeping from a jagged cut on his left cheek. The fall had injured him. Not only was she going to have to pay for his skis, but she was also going to be paying medical bills.

He reached up and pulled off his ski hat. "Are you nuts?" he shouted over the howling wind. "Where the hell was the fire?"

The force of his anger made Kylie's stomach tighten. The man was royally ticked. Not that she blamed him. She'd almost killed the guy.

"I'm sorry," she said, skidding to a stop next to him. "It was totally my fault. I didn't see you until it was too late."

"Nothing like stating the obvious." Sarcasm dripped from every word.

"I didn't think anyone would be out on a night like this."

He lifted a ski pole to point to a sign. "Are you blind? Didn't you see the signs warning you that there was a ski crossing up ahead? You're supposed to slow down when going through this section of the road."

Confused, Kylie glanced at the sign. It did indeed warn drivers of a Ski Xing. She'd forgotten about the trail, failed to see the signs as she focused on trying to keep the car on the road. How could she have missed them?

"Look, I'm really sorry. I—I take complete responsibility."

"Sorry doesn't cut it, lady."

"It—it was an accident. I was concentrating on getting around the curve."

"You were going entirely too fast for the road conditions."

She shifted uncomfortably. Okay, she was willing to admit she'd been going too fast. But what the hell was he thinking skiing at night, dressed all in black and during a freakin' blizzard?

She bit back the rush of words that threatened to spill out. Deep breath. No need to make matters worse. If there was one thing Kylie knew she was good at, it was taking the blame and smoothing things over in tense situations. She was a master at it.

"Are you sure you're all right?" She pointed to his cheek. "It looks as though you cut yourself pretty badly. You might need stitches."

He reached up and casually brushed aside the trickle of blood seeping down his lean cheek. "It's a scratch. I'm fine."

He bent down and unclasped the toe binding of his other ski, the close-fitting cling of his nylon ski pants stretching nicely over his muscular form. Kylie worked to keep her gaze off his physique and on his face. Now was definitely *not* the time to be lurking on some hot guy's body. Not after she'd almost turned him into roadkill.

"My skis are shot. You'll have to give me a lift back to the lodge."

Kylie nodded and rushed over to help him, slipping and almost colliding with him. He reached out and grabbed her elbow, effortlessly keeping her from taking a tumble. She could feel the heat and strength of his grip sink down through the thick lining of her coat and singe her raw nerve endings.

"Sorry, it's more slippery than I thought."

"All the more reason not to barrel down a road with little regard for what might be around the next curve."

His tone was clipped, impatient. He was not in a forgiving mood. The possibility of a lawsuit loomed in the back of Kylie's mind.

Lord, could her luck get any worse? She considered sitting down in the middle of the road and crying. With a whopping tuition bill due in January, she was fairly certain things couldn't get much bleaker.

But she quickly brushed aside the thought. She was made of tougher stuff than that. She could handle this.

Clenching her fists, she studied the man's face. He looked familiar. Something about the classic lines of his angular face, the strong Roman nose and dark eyebrows over bluish-gray eyes, struck a cord in her. She knew him from somewhere, but for the life of her she couldn't place him.

She stuck out a hand. "I'm Kylie McKee."

He ignored her hand and swung his skis over one broad shoulder. "Michael Emerson."

Damn! Of course, she knew him. How could she have not realized? He wasn't just Michael Emerson, he was Michael Thomas Emerson, III. His ancestors were founding members of Cloudspin Lodge.

In fact, if memory served her right, he was the current president of the lodge's board of directors. She choked back her dismay.

She could only hope he hadn't recognized her name or remembered that he actually knew her. If he did remember, Kylie knew that meant she'd have to deal with the memory of their last meeting—the night things had gone horribly wrong. The night her life had changed forever.

His life, too, no doubt.

As if on cue a frown popped up between his brows. "McKee? You wouldn't by any chance be related to Daniel McKee, would you? His daughter perhaps?"

Kylie nodded, resigning herself to the inevitable. But instead of questions, the fierceness in his eyes softened just a tad. "I was sorry to hear about your father's passing."

"Thank you."

"He'll be missed. He was a good man."

Sadness clouded Kylie's throat, preventing her from speaking. She managed a small nod.

"You've changed some since I saw you last."

She nodded again but kept silent.

What was one supposed to say to a comment like that? Of course she had changed. She'd been thirteen the last time she'd seen Michael Emerson. Thirteen and banished to a private school at her father's insistence. It had been a well-meaning attempt on her father's part to get her away from the lodge and the influence of its wealthy patrons and their out-of-control offspring.

Her father had always believed that the guests at Cloudspin were morally corrupt, people who had more money and time than they knew what to do with. How many times had he lectured her over dinner about *idle hands are the Devil's tool.* And in the end, her father had been proven right. There was no getting around the fact that Andrea Greenley's death had proved that.

In any case, her father's decision to send her away hadn't been easy on either of them. Financially or emotionally. But the financial part had been particularly hard. On a caretaker's salary, he had struggled for four years to pay her tuition to private boarding school. Even the partial scholarship she'd received hadn't provided much relief.

Lucky for him, she had inherited her mother's quick intellect and had graduated early, earning a full academic scholarship to college. Medical school had been her responsibility.

But perhaps worse than the financial debt had been the emotional distance the separation had created between father and daughter. A distance they had never completely recovered from. Kylie regretted that more than any debt she had inherited.

She watched as a smile touched the corners of Michael's mouth, deepening the interesting grooves that etched the sides of his lean cheeks.

She noted the rough, unshaven line of his jaw, a look that gave him a slightly dangerous edge. It touched off a strange sensation in her, almost as if she were thirteen again and crushing on him from afar.

Impatient, she pushed the feeling aside. No way was she going back to that place. Too much adolescent angst in there. She'd grown past all of that. Or at least she thought she had.

"You used to hang out with Gracie Greenley, right?" He cocked his head and his smile took on a teasing twist to one corner. "If I'm remembering correctly, the two of you used to climb trees and spy on us older kids. And you were the one who was always falling out of trees or tripping over rocks. Nikki Greenley was always calling you klutz, right?"

Wonderful. Why was it that when you met someone from your childhood they always remembered the embarrassing moments? Why the hell couldn't he have remembered her as having great legs or a devastating smile? Blood rushed up the sides of her neck.

"Yeah, that was me."

He studied her for a moment, and she saw a flash of something close to regret enter his eyes. "We were a pretty self-centered bunch of yahoos back then, weren't we?"

"You could say that."

"Well, you have to admit that you and Gracie were pretty relentless in your pursuit of us. Nikki hated it when her little sister turned up. I think she saw Gracie as cramping her style."

"I guess everyone feels that way about their younger siblings." Kylie shrugged. "But we only wanted to hang out with the *cool* kids."

"Oh, so you're saying that we were the cool kids, huh?"

The teasing note in his voice irritated her. Who was he kidding? Of course they'd been the cool kids. He knew that. Michael had been their leader, the instigator of all the wild, carefree parties out at the swimming hole. Parties she and Gracie would have died to have been invited to.

But Michael had always chased them off, telling them they were too young. That was until the night she and Gracie had wangled an invitation out of one of the younger boys who had taken pity on them. An invitation Kylie wished they had never accepted.

For a moment, fear tumbled around in the pit of her stomach. Would Michael want to talk about that night? Would he want to discuss how it had changed their lives?

She waited, but he turned away, glancing in the direction of her car.

"I suppose you're here to clean out your father's belongings."

She nodded. "I need to get thing boxed up and into storage. The manager told me that the new caretaker will be moving into the cottage sometime next week."

A stiff breeze whipped down the center of the road and sent chunks of snow flying off the branches of the pines. A hefty clump landed on her right shoulder and several icy chunks slid down the back of her neck. Kylie shivered.

Michael slipped off his glove and casually brushed the

snow off the back of her neck. The warmth of his fingers against her cold skin sent a shiver rocketing through her, and she knew her reaction had nothing to do with the coldness of the snow.

He glanced down at her, seeming to notice for the first time that her body was racked with chills. "Why don't we get out of this cold and into the warmth of the car. You can give me a lift up to the lodge. But I'll drive."

"I think I can manage to drive my own car," she protested.

"No doubt. But try humoring me. I'm a man and I like to feel in control."

"You should work on that," Kylie grumbled, even though she'd already decided not to argue.

She opened the hatch of the Civic, and he shoved his damaged skis into the back end, slamming the trunk shut. She opened the passenger's side door with numb fingers and climbed in.

The heat blasting out of the vents poured over her body and she breathed a sigh of relief. The ice in her veins started to melt.

The driver's side door opened and he threw his ski hat onto the console between them. Expensive with a prominent gold logo on the band and a thick, tight knit to keep out the cold. Only the best for Michael Emerson.

"I'll pay for the skis of course," she said as he slipped behind the wheel and eased the car into Low. "You'll have to let me know how much I owe you."

"No need for that. They were an old pair. I have others."

She was fairly certain he did. Many others. But replacing the skis was a matter of principle to her.

"I'd still like to pay you. The accident was my fault."

He laughed, the sound rich and deep. "You're right, it was. So if you have a real need to repay me, I'll settle for a drink when we get to the lodge. Preferably something strong enough to take the chill off."

"I think I can manage that."

She didn't add that she was only too aware that hanging out in the bar of the Cloudspin, no matter how empty the place was this time of the year, wasn't something that an employee or a member of their family did. She made a note to herself to send him a nice bottle of wine when she got back to civilization.

His hands, large and capable, gripped the wheel with ease, and she found herself shooting quick glances in his direction, studying his profile and attempting to connect her memories of the arrogant teenager with the man who now sat next to her.

He'd grown up with an easy confidence, a sense of entitlement that only the rich seemed to master.

Not that any of that surprised Kylie. Eleven years ago, when other teens she knew had fumbled and stammered their way through adolescence, Michael had breezed through with ease.

At eighteen, he had commanded the undivided attention of all the females around him, young and old alike. The women had swarmed around him like anxious bees to honey, fluttering and buzzing for his attention.

Not that Michael had shown any indication that he was bothered by all that fluttering. He'd taken it in stride. Even back then, rumors about his sexual escapades had ripped through the employees like wildfire.

But in spite of how she'd felt about his youthful behavior, Kylie kept track of him over the years, and his high profile career in photography and adventure sports had made it a relatively easy undertaking. He'd become a media darling.

She'd been unable to deny her fascination with him. She'd found herself tied to him in some strange way. Just as she had found herself tied to the other teens who had been there that summer eleven years ago—a wild pack of party animals who had lived for the moment

Although her father had sent her away shortly after that night and she had never communicated with any of the others again, Kylie had felt oddly connected to Michael and the other teens from that summer so long ago. Sometimes she felt as though they were locked in a strange time warp.

Whenever Michael had an article in *Explorer* magazine, articles with his famous scrawling signature accompanied by a perfectly drawn soaring eagle at the bottom, she had devoured them. They revealed a man hooked on perilous climbing expeditions and risky white-water rafting trips. A man who took chances with his life, a true adrenaline junkie.

But it was when the stories about the Manhattan Slasher hit the tabloids and the mainstream papers that she'd really sat up and taken notice. She couldn't help but wonder about the young man she'd known as a teen. Was it possible that he'd become the killer the papers speculated about?

Had the terrible accident they'd all been a part of created some kind of monster? Kylie knew only too well how Andrea Greenley's death had affected her.

She shifted in the seat, suddenly anxious to reach the lodge. Something told her that the sooner she completed her business and returned to New York, the safer she'd feel. The further away the nightmare of that night would be.

Glancing up, she noticed they were passing through the stone pillars leading to the main lodge. On either side of the car, elegant, multimillion-dollar homes appeared, each building strategically set among groves of towering pines.

"Does your family still own Bratton Cottage?" she asked.

He nodded, his gaze fixed on the treacherous roadway.

"So, you're staying there instead of the lodge?" She knew she was talking too fast, her nervousness revealed in a need to make conversation.

"No, I built my own place a few years ago. It's on a lot close to Bratton Cottage."

Some of the members, ones whose membership extended back to the early 1800s, had been able to lease land from Cloudspin and build their own vacation homes. Their homes were passed on from generation to generation, the leases expiring after ninety-nine years but with a clause for automatic renewal.

The less fortunate members, the ones unable to afford the exorbitant leases or the cost of building one of the obscenely luxurious homes, stayed at the main lodge.

"I always liked Bratton Cottage," Kylie said. "It was one of the few places that seemed to fit in with the surrounding scenery."

"Probably because it's one of the original cottages. It was built around the same time as the lodge. Rustic." He tossed another quick glance in her direction. "Of course, my father added a few modern conveniences in order to entice my mother to agree to summer here rather than the city. Not that she ever really minded."

Nervous, Kylie chewed on a corner of her fingernail. "I

always thought some of the newer homes were a bit pretentious. A bit too modern for the Adirondacks."

He glanced sideways at her, and embarrassed, Kylie shoved her hand back into her lap. She wondered if she might have offended him with her criticism of his friends' homes.

"I'm glad to see that you haven't changed."

"What do you mean?"

"The chewing of your fingernails and—" he reached out and turned the heat down a notch "—the fact that you were never overly impressed with people. You were never shy about speaking your mind."

She was glad he had turned down the heat. Her cheeks felt overly warm. "My father always told me to mind my tongue and keep my fingers out of my mouth."

"I'm guessing you didn't listen real hard to that particular directive."

She laughed. "You're right. But then I never claimed to be Miss Manners. Must be because I never went to finishing school."

"Good thing. A woman who speaks her mind is a person to be respected. Or so my mother always said."

"From what I remember of your mother, she wasn't afraid to speak her mind, either."

"You remember right. And for what it's worth, she would have agreed with your assessment of some of the homes. She hated to see the destruction of the lodge's natural beauty. When she served as president of Cloudspin's governing board over fifteen years ago, she insisted on bylaws that preserved and restricted the development of the land."

"I remember that. Caused quite a stir with a lot of people."

"What a lot of people don't understand is that the

wealthy have as hard a time fitting in as everyone else. They just have more money to worry about while they're mired down in their angst. Most of them get fixated on trying to impress everyone." He shifted into Low for the climb. "When I took over as president, I followed my mother's lead and enacted some pretty rigid bylaws of my own. I wanted to restrict the kinds of homes members could build. Wanted the architecture to fit in with the natural landscape."

"That must have put more than a few noses out of joint."

"Some. But when I built my place, I made sure the design didn't spoil the natural beauty." He pointed out the window to a sleek log home perched strategically on a small knoll overlooking the lodge. "That's my place."

Kylie stretched to see out the window and gave a small whistle of appreciation. "It's beautiful." She noted the soft sheen of light that seemed to form a halo above the cabin. "Skylights?"

He nodded. "My single concession to modern architecture. I like lying in bed and seeing the night sky overhead. Not possible in my place in New York. So, I made some adjustments."

The thought of him stretched out on a huge Adirondack poster bed, a brightly colored quilt tangled around his long muscular legs and the brilliant night sky overhead leaped into Kylie's brain. She glanced away, embarrassed at the unexpected direction of her thoughts.

They rounded another curve and the monstrous structure of Cloudspin Lodge came into view. She sat forward, drinking it in. She hadn't realized how much she had missed the old place.

Modeled after Adirondack hunting camps that had been

popular years ago but with a great deal more grace and elegance, the lodge was four stories high with a pitched, moss-green roof. A huge wraparound porch with a domed portico and thick white columns stretched the length of the lodge. From experience, Kylie knew the porch could accommodate a crowd of several hundred.

The main entrance to the lodge was wide, with steps leading up to the double front door. A grove of white birches lined the snow covered lawn, their bare branches strung with festive lights. They twinkled invitingly in the gathering darkness.

The windows on the first and second floors spilled a welcoming yellow light on the snowy front lawn. Wreaths and ropes of pine needles still decorated the windows and the railing of the porch.

In contrast, the upstairs windows, the ones above the second floor, were all dark, giving the upper floors a gloomy, forbidding look. Kylie figured that during the winter months, the third and fourth floors went unoccupied.

As she stared upward, she was startled to see the face of a small child pressed against the windowpane of one of the fourth-floor windows. Kylie leaned against the dashboard, straining for a clearer look.

The child's hair was long and clung close to her head, as if she had just stepped from a shower. She appeared young, age four or five at the most. She waved, her mouth open to reveal an engaging gap in the front.

Kylie lifted a hand and waved back. She wondered what a small child was doing playing alone in the dark, drafty upper halls of the hotel.

"Who are you waving at?" Michael asked.

"A little girl. She's on the top floor."

Michael leaned forward and glanced up at the hotel. "I don't see anyone."

"She's at the sixth window in."

Once Michael had rounded the curve to the front entrance, he glanced up again. He shook his head, shooting a quick glance of disbelief in her direction. "There's no one there, Kylie. You must have seen a shadow."

She leaned forward again, her gaze quickly sweeping the length of the top floor. The windows were all empty, the small face pressed to the window moments ago, gone.

The hair on the back of her neck prickled and an odd uneasiness rushed through her. Had she imagined the face?

No, she must have miscounted.

She recounted the window. No face, only eerily dark windows staring down at them.

"I could have sworn there was a little girl up there," she protested, not willing to give up so easily.

"Not possible. We keep the top two floors of the hotel closed off during the winter months—securely locked. The only people who go up there periodically are the maintenance crew to check on the pipes."

Kylie strained for another look, but there was nothing. In spite of the heat pouring out of the vents, she shivered.

Was she seeing things?

She sat back. What if the dreams, the horrible nightmares that had haunted her for so many years, were now coming to visit her during her waking hours?

She swallowed against the scream of protest that rose in the back of her throat.

Perhaps returning to Cloudspin had been a mistake.

Chapter Three

Michael switched off the engine, leaving the car parked in front of the wide steps leading to the lodge. Kylie opened her mouth to tell him that she knew this wasn't where they'd want her car parked, but he was out and rounding the front of the car, headed for her side, before she could get the words out.

She knew that she was supposed to drive around back and park in the gravel lot reserved for employees. A lot designed to keep the employees' junk cars out of view and away from the guests' Jaguars, BMWs and Caddies. Not that there would be many of those this time of the year. More like Range Rovers and Hummers.

Oblivious to her dilemma, Michael opened the door and reached down to grab her small duffel bag and tote sitting on the floor between her feet. His shoulder brushed her upper chest and sent an unexpected flutter shooting through her.

She inhaled deeply and tried telling herself the sensation was due to the cold rushing in the open door. But deep down, she knew better. No doubt about it, she was going to give Michael Emerson wide berth during her short visit.

He had slung her bag over one shoulder and extended his hand to help her out.

"That's okay, I can manage."

"Relax. I'm offering you a hand, not taking over your life." His smile was smooth and effortless. "Besides, it never hurts to accept a little help—even if it's from some lazy-ass rich boy."

"I never called you that," she protested.

"But you thought it often enough over the years."

She couldn't help but laugh. He'd pegged her. "Okay, you got me. I occasionally thought you were an insolent rich boy with entirely too much time on your hands. But I would have never called you *lazy assed.*" Not when she enjoyed that particular view so much, now and back then. She brushed the thought aside.

"You might not have ever said it, but when we were kids, your eyes told me exactly what you were thinking every time our paths crossed."

He leaned down and gazed directly into her eyes. Air stalled in the back of her throat. Damn, keeping a wide berth was going to be way harder than she'd anticipated. She reminded herself to breathe.

"Yep, your eyes are still saying the same thing—lazy-ass rich boy." He straightened up and beckoned impatiently for her to take his hand.

Resigned, she reached out and watched as her hand was swallowed up in his. His touch was delicious and wickedly hot, and it flooded down through the tips of her fingers and raced up the length of her arm. Lord have mercy. She really needed to stay outside his reach if she was going to survive this weekend.

"Sorry I was such a judgmental brat," she said as she climbed out of the car.

"Judgmental, but damn good at judging character. I *was* a lazy-ass rich boy. But thankfully, I've grown up."

He took her upper arm and directed her toward the main steps. Kylie didn't have much choice other than to allow herself to be swept along. She knew the back way to her father's cabin, but she didn't relish the thought of walking the darkened path, especially since Michael still held the keys of her rented Honda in his hand and all her belongings. Besides, she probably did need to check in and let the manager of Cloudspin know that she'd arrived.

The warmth from the front hall hit her with a glancing blow to the chest, engulfing and wrapping her in its heat. She glanced around, taking in the familiar magnificence of the massive main lobby. Things hadn't changed much.

Straight ahead stood the front desk, the ancient cage enclosing the front with the large arched opening for transactions with the front desk staff. Behind the desk were the rich wooden mailboxes, cubby holes with the room numbers carefully engraved beneath. The old-fashioned bell used to ring for service sat to one side.

The heat in the room came from the two massive fieldstone fireplaces situated on either end of the room. Wood was stacked a foot high, the flames roaring and devouring the wood as fast as whoever was tending the fires could throw on the massive logs.

Leather furniture, several couches and easy chairs, were grouped around both fireplaces, giving the guests two comfortable areas to congregate and converse. One of the areas was empty, but on the left side of the room a group of four women and two men lounged comfortably.

When she spied Michael, one of the women, a tall attractive blonde, gave out a squeal of delight. "Michael!"

She jumped up and ran the length of the lobby, throwing her slender arms around Michael's neck. Her long, shapely legs swung free as she hung onto him and laughed.

"Templer told us you were here but went out cross-country skiing. We've been waiting for you," the woman said as she pressed her lips to his ear. "We'd thought maybe you'd gotten lost in the storm."

"Hello, Nikki."

Nikki Greenley. Kylie swallowed hard. So this was Nikki all grown up. No big surprise there. She was just as poised and confident as she'd been eleven years ago. Maybe even more so, considering that the gorgeous, *knock every boy and man within spitting distance to his knees whimpering,* teenager had grown into a strikingly beautiful woman.

Kylie watched as Michael extricated himself from Nikki's embrace, his hands gently setting her back a few steps. He gazed at the blonde with a slightly perplexed expression on his face. "What on earth are you doing here?"

Nikki laughed and threw back her head, gold strands of hair flowing down to the middle of her back and an exquisite pair of diamond earrings and necklace glittering and twinkling in the light.

The jewelry might have been seen by some as out of place in the rustic atmosphere of the lodge, but Nikki wore them with casual ease. Kylie had no doubt the woman could pull off wearing the Hope diamond at a bowling alley if she wanted to.

"Actually it was Gracie's idea. She called your house the other day to talk to you about one of those charity projects she's always working on and you had already left. Hattie told her that you'd come up to the lodge."

"Still doesn't explain why you're here. If I remember correctly, you despise this place," Michael said. "Haven't you said more than once that you'd never come back here?"

Nikki waved a dismissing hand. "Oh, I say a lot of things I don't mean. You should know that by now." She smiled up at him, her voice deep and throaty. "Besides, you're always telling us how beautiful it is up here during the winter. And we were all in desperate need of a vacation. So, since Gracie was adamant that she needed to talk to you this week—" she rolled her eyes toward heaven as if praying for inner strength "—and you know only too well how Gracie gets when she's on one of her charitable kicks. The rest of us decided to tag along with her."

She glanced over her shoulder at the others clustered around the fireplace. "Right, gang?"

The woman closest to her nodded eagerly, her own pair of expensive diamond earrings twinkling. She didn't have quite the panache Nikki did to carry off the jewelry, but she was obviously willing to give it the old college try.

Next to her, the other woman and the two men added their own nods of agreement.

But the third woman sat silent, her oversize hands, reddened from the cold, lay clutched in her lap. Her shoulders, broad and knobby beneath the bulk of her wool sweater, were hunched inward, as if she were uncomfortable with the heaviness of her frame and wanted to melt into the softness of the leather chair.

She reminded Kylie of an unsuspecting buzzard who had somehow stumbled upon a flock of preening snowbirds.

But there was something vaguely familiar about the woman's hesitant expression, and when she glanced up, the soft, moss-green color of her eyes struck Kylie hard.

Gracie Ann Greenley, her childhood friend.

"Hello, Kylie," Gracie said softly.

"Gracie!" Kylie moved to greet her former friend. "It's been so long. How have you been?"

Gracie leveraged herself out of the chair, her body seeming to brace itself, as if afraid Kylie might actually embrace her. She abruptly stuck out a hand. "It's good to see you. I was very sorry to hear about your father." Her palm was damp and limp.

"Thank you." Kylie paused a moment and added, "I was sorry to hear of your dad's passing."

Gracie nodded, her gaze shifting for a brief moment in Michael's direction and then quickly away again. "Yes, it was terrible. Mother, Nikki and I were devastated. We all miss him."

Her hands dropped to hang limp at her sides, as if the revelation had taken all the life out of her.

Nikki moved to stand next to them, her green eyes sharper and clearer than her sister's, glittering with feverish interest. She didn't like being out of the loop. "You know each other?"

Before Kylie could respond, Nikki turned again toward Michael. "Who's your friend, Michael? It's hard to keep all your women straight. You really should send out a newsletter to keep us abreast of your latest conquests."

Kylie bit her bottom lip in an attempt to keep from laughing. Latest conquest? That was rich and not likely in this or any lifetime. But then, she was pretty sure Nikki knew that.

She shot a glance in Michael's direction, trying to gauge his reaction, but he seemed unruffled by Nikki's dig.

"Kylie and I bumped into each other on the way up to the lodge." His gaze met hers for one amused minute before he continued, "You all remember Kylie McKee, don't you? She and Gracie used to spy on us when they were younger."

Nikki's smile slid smoothly over sparkling white teeth. Satisfied. Predatory. Kylie braced herself for the dig.

"Oh, of course. You're the caretaker's daughter, right?"

Kylie nodded, not in the least surprised at the caretaker comment. Nikki had never been one to miss an opportunity to put a person in their place. Some things never changed.

"How are you, Kylie?" she asked.

"I'm fine, thank you." She noticed that Nikki didn't offer a hand.

"Kylie's up to take care of her father's things," Michael explained.

"Sorry to hear about your father's passing." Nikki's words carried the socially correct amount of warmth and sympathy. Not too much, not too little. She was a woman who knew how to modulate her social interactions, a person who gave little of herself but knew how to put across the right image.

"Thank you," Kylie said. "My condolences to you as well."

Nikki accepted her comment with a simple nod.

"You know the others, too," Michael interjected smoothly. "Heather Barlowe. Leslie McMasters. Steven Howe and Reggie Dumont." He went around the circle, making the introductions.

A strange sense of uneasiness settled over Kylie. What an odd homecoming. Before her, Michael included, were seven of the people who had been present the night of Andrea's death. She wondered if each of their lives had been impacted as profoundly as her own.

She greeted each with a quick nod.

Nikki turned away and latched a hand on to Michael's arm. She pulled him toward a chair closest to the fire. "Come have a drink with us. Templer said you were only going for a short run and you were gone over three hours. You must be absolutely frozen."

The circle of friends seemed to close around him and Kylie knew without anything being said that the invitation for a drink was not extended to her. Not that she expected it to be any other way. After all, she really wasn't part of their crowd. Never had been.

But Michael paused and turned back around toward her. "Why don't you join us, Kylie? You *did* promise to buy me a drink as payment for almost running me down."

Nikki raised a meticulously shaped brow. "Almost ran you down? Whatever are you talking about?"

"An accident. I darted out in front of Kylie's car. Luckily she managed to miss me."

The slow, teasing smile that pulled at one corner of his mouth yanked hard on her heart. She shoved the feeling aside. "It was a close call."

Nikki reached up and gently touched Michael's cheek. "It looks as though you were hurt. Are you sure you're okay?"

"I'm fine. Nothing a good Scotch won't take the sting out of." He glanced again in Kylie's direction, the invitation to join them obvious. "Come on, don't be a spoilsport. Join us for one drink. For old times' sake."

Kylie shot a quick look at Nikki, unable to miss the barely disguised glint of resentment in her eyes. Enough resentment to stop a charging rhino dead in its tracks. No need to guess how Nikki felt about her taking Michael up on his invitation.

She feigned a yawn. "No, thanks. I'm tired from the drive up. I think I'll just take my things out to my father's cottage and get settled in. But thanks anyway."

Michael extracted his arm from Nikki's. "Here, I'll help you out with your stuff."

"No, that's okay." She slipped the strap of one of her bags over her shoulder and hefted the other. "You enjoy your drink. I can handle things just fine."

Kylie didn't want Nikki stalking after them to restake her claim of Michael. Besides, she already knew she'd feel out of place, uncomfortable among the group congregated around the fire. She didn't want pitying looks for the caretaker's daughter.

If there was anything she didn't handle well, it was pity. Over the past eleven years, she'd learned that she was worth something. She had skilled hands and a sharp intellect. That was worth something.

"Perhaps another time," she said.

She turned and walked across the lobby. As she neared the hall, she stopped short, startled by the sound of muffled yells filtering down the main stairwell. Panicked shouts bounced off the wood-paneled walls.

"Mr. Templer! Mr. Templer!" a man yelled.

"Someone call the police!" another man shouted.

The sound of the men's footsteps on the stairs was thunderous. They were running, panicked.

Behind her, Michael and the group of guests stood and moved closer. Low mutters of concern rippled through the group.

Kylie watched as two men, dressed in kelly-green overalls, rounded the stair landing, their arms flailing and their faces twisted with terror.

Michael stepped past her. "What's the problem?"

The men ran down the final few steps and skidded to a stop in front of him.

"Call 911!" the beefier of the two men huffed, his breath harsh and strained from his wild descent.

"What is all this racket about?" a new voice demanded.

Kylie turned to see a tall, well-dressed man rush out of the office directly behind the front desk. His long face was pinched with annoyance.

She knew without introductions that he was the new manager of Cloudspin. Craig Templer.

Her father hadn't had too many good things to say about the man when he'd called to talk to her about Templer's recent hiring. He'd described the man as a tyrant and all-around boob who lacked the social graces so important to her old-fashioned father. But he'd been resigned to the man's employment because of his friendship with Michael Emerson.

Kylie had gotten her own taste of Templer's unpleasant personality when the man had contacted her two weeks ago to inform her of her father's heart attack and subsequent passing. Less than five minutes into the conversation, she realized that Templer filled the bill of heartless bastard. He didn't bother to hide his irritation when she requested he arrange for her father's body to be shipped to the city for a small private ceremony. Of course, his irritation didn't come from the fact that he was upset about missing the funeral of a trusted employee. No, Templer had considered her request an imposition.

No sooner had he grudgingly agreed to make the arrangements than he'd pumped her for specifics on when she'd arrive at the lodge to clean out her father's belongings. Apparently, in Templer's world, everything revolved around keeping the lodge running smoothly, and the fact that Kylie had lost her only living relative, a man who had worked faithfully his entire life for Cloudspin Lodge, didn't elicit any degree of sympathy.

Templer turned to the guests. "I apologize for the disturbance. Please, go back to whatever it was you were doing. Rest assured, I'll take care of this matter."

"But—but there's a dead woman in room 416, sir," the shorter of the two maintenance men blurted out. "It looks as if someone cut her up pretty bad. There's blood all over the place."

The guests, who had started to shuffle back in the general direction of the living room, stopped dead in their tracks.

"Ridiculous," Templer said, his thin lips stretching into a nervous smile. "We'll discuss this in my office."

"But—" the larger of the two men started to protest.

"*Step into my office,*" Templer ordered.

"Hang on, Craig," Michael said. "No one is going anywhere until we find out what's going on."

"Everything is under control," Templer said. "The fourth floor is closed off. No one ever goes up there except the hired help. There are no dead bodies in this hotel."

"We ain't lying, sir," the shorter maintenance man said, his round face sweaty but determined.

"It looks like it might be Molly Jubert," the other man said. He swallowed hard, his plump adam's apple bouncing up and down in the middle of his thick neck. "Hard to say though with all that blood."

"Jubert?" A frown popped up between Templer's closely spaced eyes. "You mean the maid, Molly?"

Both men nodded in unison.

"Impossible," Templer said. "Molly was sent to clean Mr. Emerson's and the Greenleys' residences." He checked his watch. "I expect her back here at the lodge in twenty minutes."

"She might have been cleaning those houses, sir, but she ain't there no more. She's upstairs dead."

Tired of the arguing, Kylie rushed to the front desk, grabbed the receiver and punched in 911. Within seconds she was connected to a dispatcher. Behind her, Templer continued to argue with the maintenance men.

Keeping her voice calm, Kylie told the dispatcher that there had been an accident at the Cloudspin Lodge and that an ambulance and police were needed.

The dispatcher told her that an ambulance and police were being dispatched and would be out at the lodge soon, warning her that things might be somewhat delayed due to the storm and hazardous road conditions. Kylie reassured the dispatcher that she understood.

As she started to hang up, Templer yanked the receiver out of her hand. "Give me that."

He put the phone to his ear, frowning when he realized the dispatcher had already hung up.

He slammed down the receiver and shot Kylie a glare, his narrow chest heaving with ill-concealed anger. "You should have waited until we checked out their story. These two idiots are notorious for drinking on the job. They probably got drunk and thought they could sleep it off on the fourth floor. They're probably seeing things."

The bigger maintenance man started to sputter in protest, but Templer's quick glance in the man's direction effectively cut him off. "Now the police are on their way out here and we have no idea if their wild story is real or a figment of their drunken state."

"We ain't drunk, sir," the bigger man protested.

"If your job means anything to you, you'll keep your mouth shut. You've disturbed the guests enough with your drunken ramblings," Templer snapped.

Kylie threw up her hands in exasperation. "For heaven's sake, who cares if they were drinking or not. If someone is injured on the fourth floor, we need to check it out. She might need medical attention."

"I agree." Michael moved closer to Kylie, his height lending her the support she was looking for in this impossible situation. "Let's stop the arguing and check the upstairs. There will be time enough later to discuss how things could have been handled better."

Templer's face flushed with anger. He didn't like being second-guessed by anyone, not even the wealthiest member of the lodge.

Michael walked over to the elevator and pushed the button. He glanced over his shoulder at Templer. "You coming?"

"Of course."

Kylie stepped forward. "I'll come, too."

"There's no need," Michael said.

"You might need someone with medical expertise. I'm a fourth-year med student."

Michael wasn't able to hide his surprise, but he recovered quickly. "You're right. Come on."

The elevator door slid open, revealing an old-fashioned metal mesh gate and the small wood-paneled box beyond. Michael pushed open the gate and stepped inside, using one finger to hold down the button to keep the door open.

Kylie eyed the cramped space, a bubble of anxiety rising inside her belly. No way in hell was anyone getting her into that contraption. Not in this lifetime anyway.

Templer and the two maintenance men stepped around her and entered the elevator. Michael eyed her impatiently.

"I—I'll take the stairs," she said.

"You'll what?"

"I'm taking the stairs. I'm not real fond of elevators."

"Fine." He stepped out of the elevator. "I'll go with Kylie. We'll meet the three of you upstairs."

Templer pulled the elevator's gate closed with a snap of his wrist and a second later the whirl of the elevator gears signaled its assent.

Kylie started up the stairs, taking them two at a time. Michael passed her easily on the right, his long legs eating up the steps effortlessly. At one point, on the second floor landing, he paused to wait for her.

As she skidded to a stop beside him, a loud clang filtered through the wall next to her. "What's that?"

"The elevator's emergency bell." Michael frowned.

"The darn thing has been acting up lately. Jack put in a new part just this morning. I thought he had fixed it."

"Are they going to be okay?"

Michael nodded. "Jack knows what he's doing. He's worked on that thing for years. He'll get it going again."

He started up the next level of stairs.

Kylie stared at the wall, a rash of gooseflesh sweeping up her arms at the thought of how close she'd come to being inside that cramped space, stuck between floors. "Shouldn't we try to help them?"

"They'll have it going again in a minute. You and I need to concentrate on helping that woman."

The reminder of the reason they were headed for the fourth floor got Kylie moving again. Of course, the woman. They needed to check on the woman.

She continued on up the stairs, shivering slightly as Michael pushed through the door at the top and entered the darkened closed-off hallway of the top floor.

The only light came from the emergency sign over the door. The sign cast an eerie red glow on the dark carpeting. Overhead, the ceiling hung low and the walls of the corridor were narrow. Claustrophobically close.

Kylie checked the brass number fixture over the door on the right.

Room 425

"Room 416 is probably about halfway down the hall on the left," Michael said.

Kylie squinted, trying to see through the thick shadows that hugged the corridor. A damp musty smell cloaked the back of her throat, and she swallowed hard, unable to prepare herself for what they'd find.

Through the gloom, she saw that one of the doors, about midway down the hall, hung open. A pale sliver of grayish light spilled out onto the floor, seeming to beckon to her.

"That must be the one," Kylie whispered.

Michael nodded and headed in the direction of the open door. But after a few feet, the dimness of the hallway slowed him down.

"There should be a light switch around here somewhere. But for the life of me I can't seem to find it."

"Me, either."

Kylie followed him, but halfway to the open door, she stopped short. Out of nowhere, a strange wall of cold slammed into her, engulfing her in a breath-stealing iciness.

Frigid fingers of cold clawed at her, pressing in on her.

She shivered, unable to shake the chill that seemed to dip down through the thickness of her sweater, causing the hair on the backs of her arms to rise.

She opened her mouth and a white vapor slipped from between her lips.

She rubbed her arms, trying to restore some warmth. "Won't your pipes freeze up if you keep it this cold up here?"

Michael glanced over his shoulder. "What are you talking about? It's not that cold. We keep it a moderate sixty degrees."

Confused, Kylie shook her head, opening her mouth to tell him that he had to be wrong. The temperature was at least thirty degrees or colder. But nothing came out. It was as if the words had frozen in the back of her throat.

She shuffled her feet and the carpet squished beneath her. She bent down and pressed the flat of her hand to the thick pile.

Strange. The carpet was saturated, the wool damp and clammy. Water squirted up between her fingers.

She leaned down for a closer look.

A tiny stream of water seeped out from the edge of the rug, spreading out across the polished hardwood floorboards.

Had a pipe burst?

Gingerly, she slid the tips of her fingers out along the smooth wood, but as she touched the liquid, the air around her seemed to magically freeze, turning the top layer of water to a crystallized sheen of white. She snatched her hand back.

What was happening?

She bent lower. Footprints were pressed into the thick weave of the carpet. Small feet. A child's footprint.

Confused, she lifted her head. It was as if a child had stood in the middle of the hall dripping wet.

What in the world was a child doing up here? And soaking wet, to boot. She would freeze in this chill.

She glanced around. Could the footprints have been made by the child she'd thought she'd seen earlier? The one who had pressed her face to the window?

It fit—the child would have been halfway down the hall, in or around room 416 when Kylie had seen her from the driveway below.

Fear swept through her. Could the maintenance men have seen a child? Was she the one injured?

No, the men had definitely said a woman. The child she had seen at the window was too small to have been mistaken for a woman.

She shoved her wet hand into her pocket, the tips of her fingers achingly cold. Where was the coldness coming from?

A quick glance at Michael told her he didn't feel the freezing temperature. He stood a few feet from her, his head tilted slightly as he watched her run her other hand over the carpet, testing the wetness.

"What are you doing?"

"I'm—I'm not sure." A strange sense of otherworldliness swirled around her, insulating her, pulling at her. It was if Michael's voice was fading in and out, coming from a long distance away.

She felt as though she were drifting, disappearing.

She shivered as the soft voice of a young child seemed to filter down the hall. But the child's voice was faint, too far away for her to make out the words.

Michael must have sensed that something was wrong because through the haze surrounding her, Kylie could see concern flash across his face.

He rushed over to her. His height in the darkness suddenly imposing. Ominous. The thick shadows of the hall pressed in on her, and the air, cold and stinging in her lungs, seemed to move with increasing sluggishness. She felt as though she could barely breathe.

She shook her head, trying to clear it, and as her brain moved to track what was happening to her, a new fear rushed through her.

She was alone in a deserted hallway with a man suspected of killing four women. What in God's name had she been thinking when she had rushed upstairs with him?

There was no one nearby. If anything happened, no one would hear her screams. She was totally and completely at his mercy. Alone with the man suspected of being the Manhattan Slasher.

MICHAEL WATCHED as fear clouded the depth of Kylie's eyes, the pupils widening and dilating with shock. She shuddered and stumbled backward, pressing her slender frame against the corridor wall, as if to melt into the dark paneling.

Concerned, he reached out to touch her, determined to gently shake her out of the strange trancelike state that had captured her.

But as soon as his fingers brushed her upper arm, she jerked away, her feet scrambling to get her beyond his reach.

He frowned. What the hell was wrong with her?

Frightened eyes met his, and he knew without her speaking that she was petrified of being alone with him. Somehow he needed to reach her. Reassure her.

"Relax, Kylie. I'm not going to hurt you. I just want to help you up."

He stepped forward and gently wrapped his hand around her upper arm. Cold seemed to emanate from her entire body. She was like a statue of ice.

She opened her mouth, but no words came out. She stared up at him mutely, her eyes wide with terror.

"What's wrong? You look as though you've seen a ghost."

Her gaze remained locked on him, but still no words passed her lips.

Michael felt an overwhelming urge to pull her to him, to press her frame against his in an attempt to warm her.

But he resisted the urge. Something told him that if he made a move to get closer, he'd frighten her even more. Better to simply stick to a reassuring voice and help her regain her equilibrium.

But she didn't give him the chance. She slipped out of his grasp and moved to the opposite side of the hall, her back pressed against the wall. She reminded him of a person going to the firing squad. Frightened. Guarded.

"I'm—I'm fine. Just cold." She rubbed her hands up and down her arms, trying to warm herself.

She nodded in the direction of the open door. "W-we'd better check out the room."

She turned and ran, reaching the open doorway ahead of him and skidding to a stop.

She gasped in horror. "Oh, God. They were right. Someone is in here!"

Michael moved in behind her and glanced around the room. A double bed occupied much of the narrow living space. The only other furniture was a small oak dresser. The heavy smell of copper hung in the air.

A woman lay in the middle of the bed, her bare legs tangled in the sheets, her arms flung out at her sides.

Michael tried the light switch on the wall to the right. Nothing. He flicked the switch a few more times but the overhead light didn't come on.

He brushed past Kylie and made his way over to the dresser. Reaching under the tiny lamp shade, he turned on the crystal boudoir lamp. A weak, hazy light filled the small room.

Behind him, Kylie gasped. The maintenance men had been right—blood was everywhere. Its rich redness soaked the sheets and splattered the pristine white walls in a wild arc over the headboard.

Michael immediately spotted the weapon, an ice climbing ax, the business end of the sharp tool buried deep in the woman's chest. The savagery of the attack was incomprehensible.

The killer had used the ax for more than one strike. The woman's chest was filled with numerous tears, gashes and punctures. She was naked beneath the sheets, her arms and legs spread wide as if in total surrender.

With a gasp, Kylie brushed past him, running for the bed. With a trembling hand, she reached out and touched the neck of the woman, searching for a pulse.

In the dim light, she glanced up at him, her brown eyes orbs of fear. Fear radiated from every fiber of her small frame.

"I can't feel a pulse," she choked.

Her movements frantic, she slid her hand to the opposite side of the woman's neck, searching to find a pulse somewhere. Anywhere.

Her finger skidded through the blood covering the woman's neck and upper chest, wetting the cuffs of her sweater. Oblivious to the blood, she bent down and pressed her head to the woman's chest, pausing to listen for a heartbeat. She shook her head.

Before Michael could stop her, she pressed her mouth to the woman's and blew in two quick breaths. She straightened up and made a fist, landing it in the center of the woman's chest, directly to the left of the buried ice ax.

"Oh please, God. Please let her be all right," Kylie begged. She pumped with renewed vigor, counting off the compressions. She glanced up at him. "Help me, Michael. We need to try and resuscitate her."

Michael moved to the bed and touched the woman's carotid with the tips of his fingers. Nothing.

The woman's skin was warm, but a bluish tint colored her lips. Her eyes were open and stared blankly at the ceiling. The total emptiness of her gaze and the wideness of her pupils testified that she was gone.

"She's gone, Kylie."

Kylie didn't seem to hear him. She continued the frantic compressions, pausing to give the woman two more quick breaths.

When she raised her head to begin compressions again, Michael noticed that blood was smeared across her lips, extending up along her cheek. She was in shock, unable to accept his assertion that the woman was dead. She again started the compressions on the woman's chest, her voice shaking as she counted.

Moving around the end of the bed, Michael came up behind her, gently wrapped his arms around her and pulled her away.

"Stop. She's gone. There's nothing more you can do for her."

Kylie leaned back against him, her body going limp. He turned her around and pressed her dark head to his shoulder. The blood on her small hands smeared across his sweater as she clutched him. She hung on tight as if needing his strength to regain her sanity.

A small sob escaped from between her lips and vibrated against his chest. He gently stroked her back, marveling at the thinness of her frame, the outline of her spine against the palm of his hand. He knew she'd suffered a lot in the past few weeks. The death of her father and now this. How could he comfort her?

Beneath his hands, her body shook.

"Who would have done this to her?" she whispered, her words muffled in the thickness of his sweater.

"I don't know. But we'll find out. But for now we need to get you back downstairs."

She froze in his arms. "We can't just leave her here like this."

He raised a hand and touched the back of her head, stroking her hair, acutely aware of its softness as he desperately tried to impart some sense of comfort. His fingers tangled in the vibrant strands and in a flash, he found himself propelled back in time.

Growing up, Kylie had always been the one to rescue the blue jay with the broken wing, taping popsicle sticks to splint the wing and tenderly laying the bird in a nest of shredded newspaper, cotton balls and paper towel. She'd spend weeks feeding the lice-laden creature from an eyedropper while scrounging for worms during the early morning hours. Other times, she'd come across some mangy stray and hide him in the gardener's shed, sneaking out after dinner to feed the mutt table scraps.

Of course, her escapades were always discovered and she was forced to give up her rescue victims. Michael remembered well her devastation even then. A scrappy little girl with tangled hair and a fierce expression of defiance who wailed with unrelenting rage when her latest project was hauled off to some unknown destination. Even then, as self-centered as he was, Michael had admired her courage. But something told him that if she was going to survive as a doctor, a person who dealt with death on a daily basis, she was going to have to toughen up emotionally.

"We can't move her, Kylie. She's dead. There's nothing we can do for her but wait for the police and paramedics."

"We can bring her downstairs where it's warm. We can't just leave her up here alone."

"There's nothing we can do for her," he repeated. "The police are going to want to see the crime scene left intact. We can't move anything until they arrive." If there was anything he'd learned over the past few months, it was how the police operated at a crime scene.

Kylie nodded, possibly understanding what he was trying to tell her but still unable to move. But as he held her, her body seemed to relax a bit in his arms and the shivering quieted to a light tremor.

Michael knew he needed to get her out of the room. If she looked in the direction of the bed again, the violent trembling would begin anew. He needed to get her downstairs where it was warmer. Brighter.

With slow steps, he guided her toward the door. "Come on, we'll wait for the police downstairs."

She kept her head averted from the figure on the bed, but her fingers dug into his upper arms as she struggled with the need to stay and help the woman.

She stumbled slightly as they walked back into the darkened hall, forcing Michael to use all his strength to keep her upright. A few feet away, the elevator door slid open and the occupants stepped out, looking at the two of them with concern.

"What happened?" Templer asked, striding to meet them. "The damn elevator kept us trapped for five minutes."

"Don't go in there, Craig," Michael warned. "The maintenance men were right. There's a dead woman in there."

"You have to be joking," Templer said angrily. He

pushed past Michael and entered the bedroom. His gasp of horror told Michael he had learned the hard way to listen.

"Who would have done this?" Templer said.

"I don't recognize her," Michael said. "But she was definitely murdered. Someone buried an ice ax in her chest. Get out of the room, Craig. The police are going to need to deal with this."

Templer backed out of the room, his face ashen.

"Everyone needs to go back downstairs. We'll wait until the police arrive," Michael instructed. "There's nothing more that can be done for her. She's been dead for a while."

An uncomfortable silence hung heavy in the hall, and the tiny group shot glances of concern in his direction. He knew without anyone saying anything just what they were thinking. As the number one suspect in the Manhattan killings, they were now considering his possible connection to the murdered woman in the room behind them.

He didn't fault them for their suspicions. Hell, even he had entertained the thought that he was somehow involved. Either the killer had followed him here or he was directly responsible for the woman's death.

He couldn't deny the strange coincidence. A coincidence that made him question his own sanity. His own innocence.

A strange heaviness seemed to seep out of every nook and cranny of the old lodge, swirling around them and engulfing them in its cloying darkness.

The headache that hadn't bothered him for the past few hours jumped to the forefront, rushing in to recreate the excruciating pain directly between his eyes, reminding him that there was no escape.

Next to him, her body still pressed tightly to his, Kylie

stared up at him, her gaze searching out his as if she was desperately trying to read his face—trying to determine if he was the type of person capable of such brutality. Such savagery.

Finally she blinked, as if willing herself to break the strange connection that vibrated between them like a live electrical wire, but she seemed incapable of looking away. Unable to break the thread of awareness that stretched so tautly between them.

But then, she shook herself and stepped back, breaking the connection. A dark coldness seemed to settle into the depths of her eyes, and her shoulders sagged as if the effort to separate from him had sapped her energy.

She turned away, shutting him out with a finality that shook him. He reached out, but she walked off down the hall.

Michael followed and the others trailed behind him. He knew that once they reached the lobby the accusations would follow, along with the arrival of the police.

He suddenly felt like there was no escape from the horrors he'd faced in the city.

Chapter Four

Kylie brushed past the group gathered at the bottom of the staircase and crossed the lobby to stand in front of the fire.

She was suffocating, her breath coming in tight, ragged gasps. Visons of the woman lying in a pool of blood flashed through her brain, crashing in and out like flicks of swirling destructive color.

Her hands shook and her fingers plucked at the sides of her pants. Somehow she needed to get a handle on the shakiness ripping through her body.

Behind her, the guests peppered Michael and Templer with questions, their voices shrill and excited. She tried to shut them out, but their voices pressed in on her.

She bent down and grabbed the poker, jabbing the metal tip into the hot coals glowing and snapping beneath the pile of logs.

"What do you mean she was murdered?" Steven Howe demanded. "We've been here all afternoon. None of us heard anything."

"The room is four flights up," Michael said. "The stairway door was shut. It's not surprising that no one heard anything."

Kylie shoved the poker into the center of the crumbling ash with a vicious jab. How in God's name was he able to come off sounding so calm? So rational? Did the man have ice water in his veins?

Her own tongue seemed glued to the roof of her mouth, sluggish and uncooperative. Even if she had wanted to say something, she was positive nothing coherent would come out.

"You okay?"

Startled, she looked up to see Gracie standing over her.

She swallowed hard and nodded, forcing words off her tongue, "I'm fine. Just a little shaken."

"Is she really dead?" Gracie whispered.

"Yes."

Gracie dropped down to sit on the edge of the hearth, her hands rushing to tuck her wool skirt around her legs. "You were brave to go up there. I don't think I could have done what you did."

"I wish I could have actually done something for her. Anything. But it was too late." Even to her own ears, her voice sounded resigned. Defeated.

She shoved the poker into the log again, watching as chunks of glowing red fell into the pile of white ash beneath the metal grate.

She was too damn sensitive, too easily affected by things. It was something she'd fought her entire adult life.

She sat back on her heels. Who was she kidding? If she was into dissecting her faults, she might as well admit she'd battled the sensitivity issue her entire life.

What made things especially hard was there was no room for emotion in medical school. No place for doubts or second guesses. Hard science and confidence was what was needed, and she had failed in the confidence department more times than she liked to admit. She had worked hard to hide that particular flaw from her professors and fellow students. Most of the time she hadn't succeeded.

Leaning forward, she shoved the poker back into the stand. Metal clanked dully against metal.

Gracie seemed to sense her despair and awkwardly pressed her hand to Kylie's shoulder, squeezing gently. The gesture was tentative. Hesitant. It told Kylie that she wasn't used to providing comfort.

"I'm sorry," she said. "It must have been so hard to see."

Kylie nodded. "What's hard is believing that one human being could do that to another. It was brutal."

She'd seen enough accident victims during her tenure in the E.R., but nothing compared to the brutality of what she'd seen on the fourth floor. She closed her eyes, attempting without much success to block the image flashing behind her eyelids.

"I'm sure you did what you could," Gracie said softly.

"Not enough. She's dead."

She reached up and laid a hand over Gracie's, trying to draw strength from her friend's gesture. They exchanged glances of understanding.

A sudden thought invaded her grief. Why hadn't she kept in touch all these years with Gracie? What had made her walk away from one of her best friends? The two of them had shared so much when they were younger. And now this.

Gracie leaned in closer. "Do you know what happened? How she died?"

Before she could respond, someone else answered, "Multiple stab wounds."

Kylie jumped slightly and glanced over her shoulder to find that Michael stood directly behind them.

In a heartbeat, his eyes connected with hers, the concern in his face palpable. Was he worried she was going to crumble?

She felt like she might, but she hung on.

"You did all that was humanly possible for her, Kylie," he said. "She was already gone."

"I know."

She glanced away and concentrated on the fire. He was too close. She was still confused by what had happened between them upstairs. How could she have felt such a strong attraction for a man after what she'd seen in that room? Maybe there was something wrong with her. No one should feel as she did after witnessing such horror.

Gracie stood up. "What are we going to do? We can't just leave her up there."

"That's exactly what we're going to do," Michael said. "This is a police matter now. No one touches anything until they arrive."

"While we're waiting for them, maybe you'd like to tell us where you were all afternoon," Templer said, walking over to stand behind one of the couches, his tone and expression confrontational.

"You know where I was, Craig. I was out cross-country skiing."

"For four solid hours in a raging snowstorm?"

"A little snow never bothered me."

Templer raised an eyebrow, his expression more than a

little incredulous. "A little snow? It was a raging blizzard out there. No one stays out in a blizzard."

"I do. I'm a good skier."

"Are you sure you weren't at your house when Molly was there cleaning it?" Templer pressed.

"What exactly are you insinuating, Templer?" Nikki demanded from across the room.

Kylie turned and watched Nikki cross the lobby, taking up a position close to Michael. The tenseness in her body stated the obvious—she wasn't happy with Templer's attack and she was ready to defend Michael at all cost.

Her stance and voice told Kylie a lot. Michael had a solid champion in Nikki Greenley. No big surprise there. For as far back as Kylie could remember, women had wanted to champion Michael. What was it about a handsome, sexy man that seemed to get women's protective nature all stirred up and roaring to his defense?

Heck, if she wanted to be honest about things, she had to admit that she had wanted to slice Templer into pieces when he'd started in on Michael a few minutes ago.

"I simply asked him where he was all afternoon," Templer said.

"Well, you're out of line. There's no way Michael was involved in the murder."

"You've got to admit that nothing happened until after *he* arrived," one of the maintenance men grumbled.

"What are you talking about?" Nikki demanded. "The rest of us arrived today. Why aren't you accusing us?"

"Hey, now, let's not get carried away," Steven said, the uneasiness in his voice obvious. "I don't know about any of you, but I don't relish the thought of being suspected of murder."

"None of us do." Nikki reached up and slipped an arm through Michael's. "I am simply pointing out that any one of us could be guilty. Including the staff."

The maintenance man who had spoken up shifted uneasily. "Didn't mean nothin' by what I said."

"How long are we going to have to wait for the police to show up?" Heather asked nervously.

There was no need for anyone to respond because the sound of approaching sirens answered her question.

As a group, they turned toward the front doors.

Kylie didn't miss the expressions of relief on all of their faces. It was as if they all believed that the arrival of someone in authority meant instant salvation. No doubt they believed the police would clean up the bloody mess upstairs and allow them all to get back to their weekend plans.

But Kylie was fairly certain things weren't going to be that easy.

She stood up and smoothed her hands down the sides of her pants, brushing off the ash that smudged the tips of her fingers.

The front doors burst open and a brisk wind caused the flames in the fireplace to dance and spark.

Five paramedics, their gear loaded on a stretcher, stepped inside, stamping their boots and shaking off the snow that clung to their clothing like crystallized sugar. Four policemen followed close on their heels.

Kylie studied the policemen. Two wore gray uniforms and Stetsons. State Troopers. The other two men wore suits under heavy winter coats. Investigators most likely, the ones who would take charge of the case.

The younger of the two investigators, a man in his early

thirties, surveyed the crowd, his gaze hard and penetrating. His lanky body seemed coiled with nervous energy. Kylie figured he'd do the talking.

The other cop was older, about sixty or so. His demeanor was calm, contained, as if he'd been on investigations like this one a million times before. He hung back, his dark, hooded eyes not missing a thing. Seconds after his arrival, his attention settled on Michael.

"I'm Inspector Robbins," the younger investigator said. His gaze rolled over the group, including them all in his greeting. "We got a 911 call reporting that there'd been a possible murder."

Kylie stepped out from behind the couch. "I was the one who made the call." She pointed to the two maintenance men. "These gentlemen were the ones who found her."

"Found who?" Robbins demanded.

"One of my staff. A chambermaid by the name of Molly Jubert," Templer said.

"And you are?" Robbins asked.

Templer pulled himself up, resorting to a bit of obvious preening. "I'm the manager of Cloudspin."

Robbins nodded, his expression unimpressed. "Where's the body located?"

"The fourth floor. Room 416," Michael said.

The older cop's smile was cold and predatory. "You touch anything, Mr. Emerson?"

"Ms. McKee and I checked on her a few minutes ago. We tried not to move anything." He shrugged. "Ms. McKee started CPR, but it was pretty clear the victim was dead. I had her stop."

"And I'm just betting you knew she was dead before you even stepped foot on the fourth floor, right, Emerson?" the older cop said.

"You insinuating something, Denner?"

"No insinuation necessary. You and I both know you have a habit of making sure witnesses don't hang around long enough to talk."

Kylie's gaze jumped back and forth between Michael and the older cop. They had called each other by name, meaning they knew each other. Their mutual animosity wasn't something either made any attempt to hide. It was apparent that there was no love lost between these two men.

Robbins nodded to the paramedics and the older cop. "Let's go take a look." He pointed at the two maintenance men. "You two found the body, right?"

The men nodded in unison.

Robbins motioned to the younger man. "You come with us. The rest of you will stay here."

He paused and then addressed the two uniformed officers. "I want one of you to come with me. The other waits with the guests. Make sure everyone is comfortable until we get back."

Although Robbins had mentioned making them *comfortable,* Kylie knew he was simply signaling the officer to make sure none of them tried to leave.

As the policemen and rescue workers headed for the elevator, Michael spoke up, "We're having trouble with the elevator. Better take the stairs."

The men carrying the stretcher and heavy medical equipment groaned. They weren't happy about the prospect of hauling their equipment up four flights of stairs, but they didn't press their luck. Their footsteps hit the wooden stairs with hollow thuds as they began their ascent.

"Why don't we all go sit down," the officer assigned to watch them suggested. "Lieutenant Robbins will talk with you as soon as he's done upstairs."

With a few muttered grumbles of discontent, the group followed Michael in the direction of the couches. From the nervous exchange of glances among the others, Kylie had a feeling that things might explode at any minute. The air in the lobby seemed to crackle with tension.

She sat in the chair furthest from Michael, trying to suppress an impending sense of dread. All she wanted was to retreat to her father's cabin, pack his things and then make a quick getaway back to the city. Anything to get away from these people and the memories they were stirring up.

"How long are we supposed to wait around? We haven't even had supper yet," Reggie grumbled.

"How could you possibly think about food at a time like this?" Gracie admonished him.

"Easy. My stomach growls and I take that as a signal to eat." Reggie dropped down onto the couch. "And since it's signaling me big time, I figure it's time to eat."

Gracie shook her head and moved to the opposite side of the room.

"Why don't you all tell me what you had planned for the weekend?" Michael said, making an obvious attempt to keep the bickering to a minimum.

"Plenty of skiing and partying of course," Nikki said, rounding the end of one of the couches and plopping down next to Michael. She slipped her arm through his again, smiling up at him. "What we didn't plan was to bury ourselves in this godforsaken place for anything less. The thought of dealing with the murder of some maid was definitely *not* on my agenda for a fun-filled weekend."

The callousness of Nikki's statement irritated Kylie and she spoke without thinking, "I'm sure it wasn't on Molly's agenda to get stabbed to death as a means of ruining your vacation plans."

Nikki raised an eyebrow in her direction and laughed. "Well, well, will wonders never cease. The meek and mild Kylie McKee actually has a backbone. Who'd have thought?"

Heather snickered, not bothering to hide her enjoyment of Nikki's put-down. Kylie felt as though she'd traveled back through time and was thirteen again. This was definitely not going to be an easy night.

"I was simply pointing out that the poor woman hadn't planned on dying, and the police are just doing their job."

Nikki's cool green gaze hit her with a glint of dislike that was startling. "And I was commenting on the fact that none of us, Michael included, was involved." She flicked back her hair with practiced ease. "Besides, women like her are always having lover's spats. She probably got some local yahoo all riled up and he didn't take kindly to her brush-off. It has nothing to do with any of us."

The *woman like her* comment sent a surge of resentment shooting up Kylie's spine, but before she could respond, Templer cleared his throat and jumped into the fray. "Mr. Emerson is the only one not accounted for during the murder."

The comment made it clear that Templer wasn't done going after Michael.

"And you're bound and determined to pin it on him," Nikki stated. "Would the fact that Michael and the other board members are getting ready to fire you have anything to do with your current level of resentment, Templer?"

Michael reached across and laid a hand on Nikki's arm. He shook his head, his message to back off obvious.

Nikki shrugged one slender shoulder. "No, Michael, I'm not going to be quiet. The man mishandled the entire restoration project and wasted millions of members' dollars. Now he's mad that he's going to get his butt canned and he wants to take you down with him."

"I don't have to listen to this," Templer snapped as he moved to leave the room.

The policeman, standing near the arch leading to the opposite side of the lobby, stepped forward to block the manager's exit. "Just take a seat, sir. No one is going anywhere."

Templer snorted in disgust, but he did as he was asked, staking out a chair close to the archway.

The cop glanced around. "Why doesn't everyone just settle down and play nice?"

Kylie watched Nikki settle back, a smug expression on her perfect features. She was totally enjoying the turmoil they were in.

"So, Kylie, how long are you planning on staying?" Nikki asked, her tone bored and disinterested.

"Overnight. I'm heading back to the city tomorrow."

"Might have trouble doing that if this storm keeps up," one of the maintenance men said.

The thought made Kylie's hopes sink lower. He was probably right. And now with the murder investigation in progress, she might have even more trouble leaving.

"You're in such an all fired hurry to get out of here, perhaps the police should be questioning you," Nikki said.

"I'm sure they'll get around to me," Kylie said softly.

"I've always heard that the hired help fight over the silliest things. Maybe you and Molly had a bit of a spat earlier."

"In case you've forgotten, I didn't arrive until after you."

Nikki shrugged and casually examined her perfect manicure. "So you claim."

"Okay, that's enough, Nikki," Michael stated.

Nikki hissed and clawed the air playfully. "Relax, lover boy, Kylie and I aren't going to get into a catfight. At least not now, right, Kylie?"

Before she could respond, one of the other cops reentered the room. "If you'll follow me, Ms. McKee. Lieutant Robbins would like to speak with you."

As Kylie stood up, Nikki shot her a triumphant look.

Kylie ignored her and walked over to the policeman. She could feel Michael's heated gaze follow her out of the room. Without question, she knew he was wondering what the police would ask her. And perhaps even more importantly, what she would say to them.

Chapter Five

The policeman walked Kylie through the archway and down the hall. "Lieutant Robbins and Detective Denner are just finishing up. They asked that you wait in the library."

They passed a door with a plaque stating, Fitness/Spa. She was mildly surprised. It seemed that Cloudspin was going modern.

But then, she shouldn't have been that shocked. In this day and age, having exercise equipment and a whirlpool for the guests was a must.

Maybe Nikki had been wrong. Perhaps Templer's renovations weren't as off the mark as she had alluded to a few minutes ago.

At the end of the hall, the policeman opened the library door and stepped aside to allow her to pass.

Before she could turn to ask him how long she'd have to wait, the cop closed the door and left. She was alone.

Restless, an uneasy gnawing sensation niggling in her belly, Kylie moved to stand in front of the bank of windows overlooking the side yard.

In the summer, the place hosted a world class croquet court. Now nothing of the smooth grassy court existed. In its stead stood mountains of snow, the mounds getting higher with each snowflake that fell from the dark, moody sky.

No one needed to tell her that the storm was worsening. The intensity increased with each passing moment. Inches of the thick, fluffy stuff fell with a vengeance, making it seem as if it would never end.

Overhead the sky hung low and ominous, not a star in sight. Occasionally the snow would change to sleet and the pellets hit the windows with a sharp ping, warning of more to come.

Kylie reached out and pressed her palm against the center of the window. The glass immediately cooled the heat of her palm and stopped the trembling that until now had seemed unstoppable.

She leaned forward and rested her forehead against the cold glass, taking solace in its coolness. A slight headache had started as soon as the policeman had escorted her into the massive room.

One by one the police would isolate each of them, getting them alone for questioning. Kylie realized that it was all so similar to how things had been handled eleven years ago when Nikki and Gracie's little sister had died at Mannahu Falls. The police had come and questioned each of them alone.

Even then Kylie had felt the isolation and terror of the police interrogation. She had read the suspicion and disbelief in the expressions of the local cops, and the fear and disappointment on the face of her father. All the memories of that time came crashing back with a crushing heaviness.

She turned away from the window. What were the police going to want to know this time? She'd just arrived at the lodge. She didn't even know the woman who had been murdered.

She glanced around the room. The mahogany shelves lining the walls were filled with books, many of them appearing to be first editions. On one wall hung a collection of framed articles. Closer inspection revealed them to be about or by the lodge's various members. A trophy wall of sorts.

Curious, she stepped closer, not in the least surprised to see that a fair number of the articles were ones written by Michael. His scrawled, looping signature and the trademark line drawing of the soaring eagle were clearly visible at the bottom.

Two of the articles made her smile. They were old newspaper columns clipped from Keene's local newspaper. The dates indicated they'd been written more than thirteen years ago. Michael had written critiques of several local climbing events. Even back then, Michael had the distinctive signature and the trademark eagle. His flair for the media had developed early.

She drifted over to the giant fieldstone fireplace and gazed appreciatively at the craftsmanship. No question that it was her father's handiwork. The meticulous balance of color in the stones revealed her father's innate artist's flare.

She leaned closer and smiled as her fingers traced the outline of a single stone laid lovingly in the center over the fireplace opening. It had been her choice. A pinkish colored sandstone in the shape of two hearts interlocked. The find had created a childish delight in her, and her father had placed it in the center of the fireplace, giving it a position of honor.

As a child, age six, she had sat for hours watching her father rebuild the fireplace, listening in rapture as he explained the art of finding just the right stone, the perfect color, shape and balance to complement the other stones.

Kylie hadn't realized at the time that her father had been passing his love of his craft onto her, the lost art of stonemasonry. It had been a while since she had worked on a fireplace, but she knew without question that the procedure was imprinted on her brain. It had been her father's legacy, a true gift.

"Ms. McKee," a voice said from behind her. "We have a few questions for you."

Kylie whirled around to find Robbins and Denner standing shoulder to shoulder in the doorway. It was the younger cop who had spoken.

"Please, take a seat. Make yourself comfortable."

Kylie did as she was told, wondering how anyone was suppose to make herself *comfortable* in the midst of a murder investigation.

She perched on the edge of one of the easy chairs situated close to the fireplace and clasped her hands in her lap, pressing her palms together in hopes that the two men missed the fact that she was trembling.

"Mr. Emerson mentioned that you were with him earlier this evening."

"Y-yes, that's true. We met on the road leading into the lodge. I'm not used to driving on the icy roads, and I lost control of the car and almost ran him down."

She paused a moment and then continued, "That's how he got the cut on his cheek."

"How exactly?" Robbins asked.

"My car wheel clipped the end of one of his skis and it threw him forward into a snowbank."

"And you think that explains the cut on his cheek," Denner asked.

Kylie nodded. "Yes, he was going pretty fast, trying to get out of my way. I think he realized that I'd lost control of the car. His momentum threw him into a snowbank facefirst."

Denner moved closer, looming over her, using his size in an obvious attempt to intimidate her.

"You're positive the cut on his cheek was caused by the fall?"

"Yes, I'm sure it was caused by the fall." She frowned. "A-at least I think I'm sure. I mean, I didn't really see him up close until after I got out of the car. But it was bleeding like a fresh cut."

Denner smiled. "So, you're not really sure. You just *assumed* it was caused by the accident."

Kylie realized he was pressing this issue so hard because he wanted to determine if the scratch on Michael's cheek could have been caused by a struggle with the murdered maid.

She stiffened. Suddenly she wasn't as intimidated as she was a few minutes ago. Denner was getting to her and not in the way he'd hoped. "I'm fairly certain that there was no visible injury to Mr. Emerson's face until after I lost control of my car and almost ran him over."

Denner changed tactics when he didn't get what he wanted. "Didn't you find it strange that a man was out skiing in the middle of snowstorm?"

"Yes, but then I'm not the sports enthusiast that Mr. Emerson is. Are you?"

"Did he appear worried? Rushed?" Denner asked, ignoring her dig.

Kylie tried a laugh. It came out sounding slightly strangled. "I'd be looking pretty worried if I looked up and saw an out of control car barreling right for me."

"Your amusement seems a bit out of whack, Ms. McKee. This is a serious investigation," Denner said, admonishing her.

"I'm sorry, I wasn't trying to be amusing," Kylie said, stung by the man's inference that she was callous. "I'm simply nervous."

"Of course you are and we're not here to make things worse for you," Robbins said smoothly, shooting a quick look of caution in Denner's direction.

Denner didn't seem in the least bothered by the investigator's glance, but he changed tactics again. "What brings you here to Cloudspin? Are you part of the group that arrived for a bit of adventure?"

"No, I know the other guests but we're not friends. I came to clean out the caretaker's cottage—it was my father's until he died recently."

Denner raised an eyebrow. He was surprised. Kylie got the impression he was a man who didn't appreciate being surprised. "So you don't run in the same social circles as the other guests?"

"No, and I'm not a member of the resort. I lived here years ago as a child. That's how I know the other members. We haven't spoken in over eleven years."

"Where do you live?" Denner asked, his question quick and clipped. He was back to trying to intimidate her.

"New York—the Bronx to be exact."

"And what do you do?"

"I'm finishing my fourth year of medical school at Columbia."

"How long have you known Mr. Emerson?"

"We knew each other as children—I lived here on the estate with my father and Mr. Emerson used to vacation here with his family. I can't say we are or were close friends."

Denner leaned in closer, his voice softening. "Yeah, I can understand that. The rich don't associate with the hired help, do they?"

Kylie knew the cop was changing his tactics again. This time making an attempt to align himself with her.

"He was a guest here. I was the daughter of one of the employees. He was always polite toward me."

"You both live in the city. Isn't it possible that the two of you ran into each other once in a while?" Denner pressed.

"As I mentioned, Mr. Emerson moves in a different social circle. And I happen to be pretty busy with my schoolwork. Getting out and socializing isn't a priority with me at this point in my life."

"No quiet dinners or secret little meetings to reminisce about old times?"

"I already told you that I haven't seen or heard from Mr. Emerson in over eleven years."

"Back off, Denner. She's answered your question," Robbins inserted smoothly. His expression softened. Kylie wondered if they were playing good cop, bad cop with her.

"Can you tell us how long the two of you were together out on the road earlier this evening?" Robbins asked.

"I can't say for sure. But I'd guess thirty or forty minutes from the time we met until our arrival here at the lodge."

"You realize, don't you, that Emerson is the prime suspect in the Manhattan murders?" Denner asked.

She shrugged. "I read the papers. Watch the news. But since he hasn't been charged with anything, I'm guessing that you don't have the evidence to support your suspicions, right?"

The lines around Denner's mouth deepened. He didn't like her challenging him. "We're building a case, and I figure I'll get what I need on him."

"Well, until then I assume he's still innocent in the eyes of the law, right?" She didn't wait for an answer, but instead, stood up and turned toward Robbins. "Are we done? I have nothing more to add."

Robbins raised an eyebrow in Denner's direction. "I don't have anything else. You?"

"I'd like to know why she's protecting him."

A flash of irritation surged through Kylie, but she squashed it as quickly as it came. Nothing good would come from antagonizing the man. He was a control freak and she'd didn't need to alienate him any more than she already had.

"I'm not *protecting* him. You asked me what time I met Mr. Emerson and I told you. I can't help it if I can't give you any more than that."

Denner stepped closer, the smell of his breath hot and sour. "He's killed four other women, Ms. McKee. Four intelligent, beautiful women who did nothing more than trust and love him. Doesn't that frighten you? Doesn't that make you want to see him held accountable?"

"I'd want any killer held accountable. But you've already admitted that you don't have the proof to hold Michael Emerson accountable for these murders. And I resent you trying to pressure me into saying something that isn't true. I don't plan on lying simply to help you make a case."

She headed for the door leading to the hall. She paused with her hand on the knob. She turned slightly to address the two cops. "If I remember correctly, the other four women were having a relationship or had a relationship with Michael in the past. Why would he suddenly murder Molly Jubert, a woman he didn't even know?"

"I was wondering the same thing," Robbins said.

Resentment twisted the corner of Denner's mouth. "What makes you think he wasn't having a relationship with her?"

"He admitted as much."

"And you feel the need to believe a man who's dodged every attempt to come clean about his involvement with the other women?"

"I don't see it that way. From what I've read he's been very honest that he was romantically involved with the women. He just stated he didn't kill them."

Denner snorted with disgust. "You're a fool."

"Perhaps you're the fool, Detective. Trying to force evidence to fit your preconceived notion of what happened isn't what I'd call good policework."

From Robbins's direction came a small chuckle. The younger cop seemed to enjoy her mixing it up with his crony.

Before Denner could add anything else the knob of the door twisted beneath her fingers. She stepped back to allow a uniformed trooper to enter.

"Excuse me, miss. Lieutenant?"

"What's up, Miller?" Robbins asked.

"We did a search of the Emerson and Greenley residences."

"Find anything of interest?"

Miller glanced in Kylie's direction. She knew he was waiting to make sure it was okay for her to overhear what he had to say.

"Go ahead," Denner said. "The lady thinks Emerson is as innocent as a newborn baby. Let her hear what you found."

"The Emerson residence was clean. No sign the maid ever stopped there. She probably met up with the killer before she had a chance to go there."

Denner swore softly under his breath and Kylie had to suppress the desire to shoot a triumphant grin in his direction.

"And the Greenley house?" Robbins asked.

Miller pulled a small black notebook out of his pocket. "That's a different story. Downstairs, someone pulled all the dust covers from the furniture. I figure that was the maid, meaning that she went there first. In the master bedroom, we found several drops of blood on the corner of the nightstand drawer and another smear on the sheets—down along the side of the mattress."

"So, the maid was in the Greenley house and was then moved up here to the hotel once she was knocked out," Robbins said.

Miller nodded and checked his notes. "The crime scene guy thinks that she must have been making up the bed when someone attacked her from behind. I checked with the coroner and he said that he found a nasty bruise on the back of the victim's head. Figures it came from a blow from some kind of blunt object."

"Any guesses on what the blunt object was?" Denner pressed.

Miller grinned. "Better than a guess. The guys found a

bookend with some blood and hair on it underneath the bed. Killer must have dropped it after braining the woman." His smile disappeared and he shrugged. "Unfortunately there doesn't seem to be any fingerprints on it. The killer either wiped it clean or wore gloves."

"Any idea if the bookend is from the house?" Robbins asked.

"It's a match with a bookend found on the bookshelf right as you enter the bedroom—eye level. Killer must have grabbed it when he walked in on the woman making the bed. Victim never knew what hit her."

He glanced down at his notes again. "The CSI guys figure that the blood on the drawer and the bed got there when the maid fell. She must have clipped the edge of the drawer when she went down."

Bile rose in the back of Kylie's throat.

"Anything of interest in the nightstand?" Robbins asked.

Trooper Miller shook his head. "Nah, just a few pens, a couple sheets of writing paper, hair clip, nail file. Some loose change. We found an old photo album behind the stand, must have slid off the stand and fallen back there."

"Not much," Robbins stated, his disappointment evident in the tone of his voice.

Miller smiled again. "Don't despair. I saved the best for last."

"And that is?" Robbins demanded.

The trooper pulled a small evidence bag out of his pocket and held it up. "We found a photo crumpled up in the victim's hand. I checked the photo album we found behind the nightstand and there's a spot near the back that most likely held the photo—it fit perfectly." He turned the bag over. "Looks as though something was slipped into a small pocket taped to the back."

"Like what?"

The trooper shrugged. "Don't know. Whatever was in there is gone now."

Denner held out his hand. "Let me see that."

Miller glanced at Robbins, again checking with his boss before complying with Denner's demand. Kylie didn't miss the flicker of resentment that slid across Denner's face. The man didn't like playing second fiddle to anyone.

Robbins ignored Denner's irritation and motioned for Miller to hand him the photo. Apparently, in spite of being willing to allow Denner to participate in his investigation, Robbins wasn't about to let the New York City detective hijack his case.

He examined the photo and then handed it to Denner. The older cop studied it for a minute and then glanced at Miller. "Anyone know who the kid is?"

Miller shrugged. "No, but we haven't asked any of the guests yet. Since it was in the Greenley residence, I'm guessing that one of them will know who she is."

Denner's gaze settled on Kylie. He extended a hand toward her, offering her a look. A small tremor of fear gnawed at her. Something told her she didn't want to see the picture, but she walked over to the detective and accepted the plastic evidence bag.

Taking a deep breath, she glanced down. Her heart thudded hard deep inside her chest and the tips of her fingers went numb.

"You know who she is, don't you?" Denner said.

Kylie nodded, unable to look up. She ran her finger across the plastic sheeting covering the photo. The bag was still warm from sitting in the trooper's pocket.

"So, who is she?" Denner demanded.

"It's a picture of Grace and Nikki Greenley's younger sister, Andrea. She died eleven years ago from a fall. She was only five."

"I remember the case. I was about twenty at the time," Robbins said. "The little girl fell from the cliffs—a place where the local teens used to swim and party. Real sad situation. If I remember correctly, it caused quite a stir around here."

"Wonder what it has to do with this whole case?" Denner said.

"Good question." Robbins stuck the evidence bag in his pocket.

"Are you done with me?" Kylie asked again.

Robbins nodded absently and motioned for her to leave.

THE HALLWAY was cloaked in darkness, the only light was a tiny sliver filtering out from beneath the library door. A cloying dampness hung close to the floor, seeping through the soles of his shoes and chilling his feet.

Michael shifted in his seat, the hard wood of the chair pressing against his lower back. He leaned his head against the wall behind him and stared blankly at the opposite wall in the shadowy alcove.

A moose head, stuffed and mounted, hung there. Its eyes, glassy and transfixed, stared directly into his. The damn thing gave him the creeps.

"I'm guessing from your appearance that you've already met Detective Denner," he said half joking, half serious, his voice echoing in the empty hall.

Lucky for him, the moose didn't respond.

He reached up and rubbed the sore spot between his eyes. The headache was back with a vengeance. Reaching down, he patted his pants pocket. Empty. He'd left the pain pills in his ski jacket. He sighed.

Maybe that was for the best. If he was going to have to face Denner, he was going to need his wits about him. He didn't want to end up looking like the damn moose, hung up to dry.

He leaned forward and glanced down the hall in the direction of the lobby. The trooper still stood at the other end, his back to Michael. The sound of the others sitting in the lobby filtered down the hall, muted. Distant.

The trooper had escorted Michael to the alcove shortly after Denner and Robbins had disappeared into the library to question Kylie. He figured that Denner wanted him segregated from the others for a reason.

Most likely the detective didn't want him talking to anyone, influencing their statements in any way. And as usual, Denner probably wanted the first shot at Michael. These interrogations were getting too familiar.

The library door's knob rattled and the heavy oak door swung open. Light spilled out into the hall in a large yellow slice. Michael sat up.

Kylie stepped out into the hall, her dark lashes brushing the crests of her pale cheeks as she blinked to adjust to the dim light. He could tell that she hadn't yet seen him sitting off to the side. She seemed distracted, lost in some deep inner thoughts. Thoughts no doubt stirred up courtesy of Detective Denner.

He had forgotten over the years how beautiful she was. How unique. Her dark brows were arched over sorrowful brown eyes, eyes so deep and soulful that they seemed to speak all on their own. But it was her expressive mouth with its full bottom lip that he remembered the most.

He smiled to himself. Years ago, he and the other randy teens who had roamed the grounds of the lodge had laughed about how kissable those lips had seemed. Too full and ripe to belong to an innocent thirteen-year-old girl with a body to match.

But when a few of the other boys had threatened to go after the *little piece of jail bait,* Michael had warned them off, telling them that Daniel McKee would come after them with a shotgun if they tried anything. But in reality, he hadn't been concerned about her father, he'd been concerned about one of his obnoxious friends hurting the sweetness he knew resided in the caretaker's young daughter.

As he watched her now, he saw her upper teeth work that lush bottom lip, worrying it with an intensity that told him if she kept it up, she'd have a nice bruise there by morning.

The expression on her face was a mixture of anger and confusion. Tiny lines bracketed the corners of her exquisite mouth, and she held her body rigid as if she were afraid she might crumble into a million pieces at any moment.

Denner had obviously worked her over good, turning her upside down and inside out. The knowledge bothered him, made him want to confront the man with a familiar protective vengeance, the same protectiveness that he'd felt all those years ago.

But something told him that his reaction wouldn't do

much when it came right down to it. He knew Denner only too well. The man was determined to find a way to pin the maid's murder on him, and if that meant forcing the others, Kylie being at the top of his list, to reveal information putting him at the right place at the right time, then Denner would.

Michael knew he wasn't responsible, that he hadn't anything to do with the woman's death. He'd been conscious of every moment during the day. There were no blank times, no missing pieces.

"You look like they put you through the wringer," he said softly.

Her gaze snapped in his direction, surprise replacing the confusion that had been there a minute ago. "What are you doing sitting here in the dark?"

"Waiting my turn for them to push bamboo shoots under my fingernails." He stood up, pushing aside the stab of pain that hit him directly between his eyes. He hoped he'd get through the interrogation without keeling over. Showing Denner any sign of weakness would be a big mistake.

"I gather they're done with you."

She smiled sadly. "More than done. I can honestly say I've been sufficiently sliced and diced by experts."

"Sorry you had to go through it."

Her gaze touched his face, there was no missing the sorrow in the deep brown of her eyes. "Not your fault."

She walked over to stand a few inches from him. The fear he'd seen earlier in the hall upstairs was gone. She'd conquered that, put it behind her.

"You do realize, don't you, that he's after you with a vengeance?"

He knew without her saying so that she was referring to Denner. "He has been for a while."

"I told him that you were with me from the time we met up on the access road until we arrived here to find the body."

"I appreciate you backing me."

She shrugged. "I simply told the truth. Not that he seemed to believe any of it. He definitely has it in for you."

"He has his reasons."

"What are they?" She frowned and added, "Wait, you don't have to say anything. I didn't mean to pry."

"You're not. The murders in Manhattan have all been tied to me in some way."

"I know. I've read the papers."

He reached up and rubbed the aching spot between his eyes.

"Are you all right?"

"Just a headache." He smiled ruefully. "Had a pretty bad climbing accident several months ago, lost a good friend. I haven't completely recovered."

He didn't add who he'd lost or how responsible he felt for that loss. No sense. He didn't have the ability to change the past. No one did.

"Did you suffer a concussion?"

He nodded. "But things are getting better."

"Still, I'm sure the fact that I almost ran you over didn't help matters any. Didn't your doctor tell you to take it easy on the physical stuff for a while?"

"Sure. But I don't slow down easily."

"Why am I not surprised? Let me guess, you're not what we call in the business a compliant patient."

He grinned. "Depends on the doctor. Want to take over my case?"

"No, thanks, I'm just a med student." She dropped down into the seat he'd just vacated. "What's going on, Michael? Why are all these women being killed?"

"That's the million-dollar question and I don't have the answer. Wish I did."

"All the women have something in common with you, right?"

"They were all good friends or women I dated—with the exception of Molly. I never met her."

"They found a picture of Andrea Greenley in Molly's hand. They seem to think that it's some kind of clue."

Frowning, Michael slipped into the seat across from her, their legs so close that he could feel the heat radiating off her. "Andrea? Little Andrea who fell off the cliff?"

Kylie's hair, thick and vibrant, moved hypnotically with the nod of her head. His hand itched to reach out and touch the curling strands, to see if they were as soft as they appeared.

"What do the other women who were killed have in common with you, Cloudspin and Andrea Greenley?"

"Nothing." He paused a moment, thinking. "Well, that's not exactly true. They've all come here at one time or another. Most—no, all—when they were younger. Vacations with their parents. Hell, most of them probably attended that fateful party at the cliffs eleven years ago."

Kylie's dark eyes bored into his. "You mean all the other women were members of Cloudspin?"

"Mostly their families." He shrugged apologetically. "I'm so busy with my job that I never get around to meeting a new group of people socially. Most of my time is spent hanging out with climbers and photographers overseas. So when I come home to roost I see mainly the people I've known since childhood."

"This is significant, Michael." She reached out and grabbed his hand, her excitement obvious. "You need to let Robbins and Denner know."

He liked the feel of her hand in his, her fingers light and cool, her grip sure. He didn't want the moment to end.

"I can't imagine they don't already know about the connection. The women's lives—my life—has been investigated from every conceivable angle."

"It's too important not to mention," she said.

"Mention what?" a voice interrupted.

Michael looked up to see Denner standing in the doorway.

Kylie stood up, her eagerness evident in the way she moved quickly in the direction of the police detective. "Did you know that all the women killed were in some way connected to Cloudspin? That they have all visited here at one time or another?"

Denner snorted dismissively. "Yeah, and that means what exactly?"

"It connects the murder victims."

"Are you trying to tell me my job?"

"No, but—"

"Good. Because I don't need your input. The fact that all those women dated Michael Emerson is a lot more important than the fact that they all vacationed here in this little playground for the rich and filthy rich when they were kiddies."

"But—" Kylie started.

"But nothing. I have a good feeling for how things fit, and my feeling is that your good friend Michael Emerson is the key."

Michael wasn't surprised when the cop's smarmy smile turned on him again. "Come on, Emerson, come clean. You came up to the lodge for a little trashy fun with the locals. Unfortunately, Ms. Jubert decided she wasn't interested in playing along and things got rough. Took you by surprise, didn't it?"

"You're barking up the wrong tree, Detective," Michael said.

"Not a chance. Why not come clean and free everyone up to go home."

Kylie stepped between them, her agitation obvious. "Look, this isn't getting you anywhere. Why won't you at least consider what we've told you?"

"Because you haven't told me anything I don't already know."

Denner waved a hand, his annoyance at her perceived meddling obvious. "I don't have time to listen to any more of this. Go to bed or sit in the lobby with the others. We're done with you tonight. I have business with Emerson."

He motioned Michael into the library, but turned to give Kylie one last parting shot. "Believe me when I say that we're not in the least interested in discussing Emerson's lurid past here at Cloudspin. Frankly I'm a hell of a lot more interested in the trashy condition of his current love life. Don't make yourself part of it!"

He closed the door with a finality Kylie found disheartening.

Chapter Six

She was dreaming, standing on the cliffs, her bare toes curled over the edge of the warm rock ledge. At her feet lay a blanket of white petals. Daisies scattered like tiny raindrops on the warm stone.

A summer breeze, hot and restless, brushed her cheeks and whipped her hair back over her shoulders.

She knew without looking what she was wearing. Her bathing suit. The soft, petal-pink bikini she'd been so proud her dad had allowed her to buy. The kind of suit the other girls had been wearing since they were ten, and her dad had resisted so vehemently for so long.

She was never sure why he finally gave in and let her buy the suit. Probably because he'd gotten tired of the endless arguments, the sullen pouts that went on for days. But in the end she'd come home from K-Mart, the suit tucked under one arm and a triumphant smile on her lips. She'd been positive Michael Emerson would notice her if she wore that suit. He hadn't.

In the dream, her shoulders were bare, warmed and soothed by the sun setting over the tops of the distant mountains. Behind her, the forest needles rustled and whispered, and the dry field grass gently whipped the backs of her bare legs. She was alone, poised to jump into the rushing river below.

She shivered, a sense of fear invading the peacefulness of the dream.

How many times had she dreamed this dream?

Ten? Fifty? A hundred times?

Things always started out the same—sweet and dreamy. Soft and comfortable like a welcome cup of ice-cold, tart lemonade on a hot summer's day. But Kylie knew only too well that things would change, morph into something dark and scary. Something terrifying.

Beneath the comforter, she moaned and turned onto her side. If she could only wake up. Stop the dream before things started to change.

But even as the thought drifted across her consciousness, she knew there was no escape. She was trapped. Caught in something determined to run full course. Only after she'd reached the end of the dream would she find release.

Her toes curled beneath the blanket, cramping in anticipation. She knew what came next and terror raced through her unchecked.

She looked down.

Cold, clear mountain water swirled and rushed over the rocks below. White foam bounced and jumped off the rocks, beads of silver in the dying light of sunset.

Her knees trembled. She was afraid. Too chicken to jump.

How many times had she watched the others take a running leap out into the center of the canyon, their strong, muscular bodies flashing tan in the sunlight right before they dropped like human torpedoes into the water below? Too many times to count.

But fear ate at her gut, kept her from jumping.

No matter how many times she approached the cliff, determined that this time she would jump, she was never able to do it.

A sharp wave of dizziness hit her and she closed her eyes. Wake up. Please wake up, she begged, the sound vibrating inside her head.

But she slept on, waiting and knowing what came next.

And finally it came.

"Kylie! Kylie! Help me, Kylie!"

The voice, clear and high, rose up over the roar of the water, and in her sleep, she trembled and opened her eyes.

The sky had turned black, as if the sun had suddenly dropped like a rock over the mountains, plunging the world into night.

Her stomach pitched and rolled and she looked down, already knowing what she'd see.

The child clung to an outcropping of rock a few feet below, her short legs scrambling frantically for footing. Her toes, sweet and chubby, bled as they scraped the sheer rock wall.

"Kyyyyyyylie! Help me! Please don't let me fall."

A bolt of nausea hit her hard almost doubling her over.

Andrea.

She needed to help Andrea.

She dropped down, stretching to reach over the edge. The roughness of the rock grazed her exposed belly, but she ignored the pain and reached for the child.

Her fingers clamped onto the little girl's wrist, and she

marveled at how small the child's arm was. So frail. So vulnerable.

Andrea's fingers fumbled to hang on, trying desperately to curl around Kylie's wrist.

"Hold on, Andrea! Hold on!" Kylie called.

The wind increased, whistling and screaming in her ear, kicking up dust and sand from the rocks and crevices, throwing it up in her face.

She wiggled out farther.

Blue eyes, wide with fear and infused with trust, stared up at her. They begged for rescue, pleaded for safety.

"Don't drop me, Kylie. Please don't drop me."

Tears welled up in Andrea's eyes and her voice shook and caught in the back of her throat.

Kylie pulled, using every muscle, every fiber of untapped strength to yank the little girl back up over the lip of the ledge.

"Don't let go, Andrea! Hold on, sweetie!" she begged, her breath coming in harsh frantic gasps.

Kylie's palm, slick with sweat, slipped over the little girl's smooth skin and her body dropped half an inch.

Andrea whimpered and then threw back her head to scream. The sound, shrill and filled with terror, echoed off the canyon walls.

Trickles of sweat dripped down the side of Kylie's face and splashed on the rock beneath her chin. Her arm ached and her fingers cramped.

Andrea twisted and thrashed as she struggled to keep from falling. Her legs twirled out into space and bounced back against the rock.

Kylie dug her toes into granite and pulled.

A few more inches. Just a few more inches and Andrea would be safe.

But the little girl slipped another inch, her fingers clawing and clutching.

"Please, Kylie," she wailed. "Please don't let me fall."

But then, Kylie felt the little girl's body go limp, as if she had suddenly given up. Called it quits.

Tiny fingers slid another fraction of an inch down the length of her hand.

Oh God, she was losing her.

Blue eyes, sad and knowing, wise beyond their years, gazed up at her. Andrea knew. She knew Kylie would fail her.

And in that instant, she was gone, falling and tumbling out into space, her tiny body snatched by the howling wind and propelled downward into the darkness.

"No!" Kylie screamed.

A spray of water and Andrea disappeared beneath the rushing current.

She scrambled to her feet. She had to jump. Had to save Andrea. But the wind and the height made her dizzy, and she stepped back from the ledge.

She let her die. Let Andrea face death alone.

She sobbed and jerked awake.

The room was dark and still, and she trembled so hard her muscles ached.

Perspiration covered her with a chilling dampness, and she sucked in warm air, trying to breathe, trying to orient herself.

A dream. It was only a dream.

She rolled onto her side and swung her legs off the edge of the couch. She sat up, tugging on the blanket and draping it over her shoulders. The embers in the fireplace glowed dark red.

"It's 2006, not 1995," she whispered softly into the stillness of the room. "You're okay. You're safe. Just a dream."

But even that reassurance, that attempt to ground herself, didn't provide the comfort or security she sought.

It never did. She'd never been able to forgive herself and there was no comfort from guilt. No hiding place from blame.

Strange, she had never seen Andrea fall. She'd been a short distance away, her face warmed by the bonfire they'd started earlier, the sounds of a guitar and soft singing filling her ears until the scream broke the mellow mood that had settled over the group.

Andrea had died all alone, her broken body found later that night, washed up on some rocks farther downstream, by the local rescue team. But Kylie had never forgotten that she and Gracie had promised to watch the little girl, and her death was testament to their failure. They'd allowed her to die alone and afraid.

The clock in the corner chimed 3:00 a.m. She pulled the blanket higher as the trembling lessened, fading to a slight inner quiver that swam in the pit of her belly.

She leaned down and gently rested her cheek on her knees.

Would she ever be free of the nightmare? How many years was she to be relegated to dreaming the same horror? Wasn't eleven years enough time for her to have forgiven herself?

"Kylie."

She glanced around the darkened room. Needles of dread marched up the center of her spine. Was she still dreaming?

"Kyyyyyyyylie."

She stood, the blanket sinking to the floor, tangling around her feet.

The call came from outside, a voice so high and clear that it rode over the wind that rattled the windows of the tiny cabin.

In a daze, she moved to the window.

Outside, the snow fell so thick that she couldn't see more than a few feet. It swirled and danced among the dark branches of the pines, and the wind dipped down, sending fine sheets of the white stuff racing across the small clearing and pushing it up against the foundation of the hotel, obscuring the walkways. The drifts were waist high.

The wind howled and the trees groaned in protest.

"Kyyyyyyylie."

She pressed her face to the window and shifted her gaze toward the small opening in the pines at the back of the cabin, the trail leading to the cliffs.

The hairs on the back of her neck rose.

A small figure, a child, stood in the clearing.

She raised an arm in greeting, and Kylie's fingers, frozen and numb, tightened against the hardwood of the windowsill. What was a child doing out on a night like this?

She was dressed in what looked like a bathing suit, a sweet little blue bathing suit with red trim. Her skin was white, totally exposed to the bitter wind and blowing snow.

My God, she was going to freeze out there.

The child waved, her thin arm lifted and beckoned for Kylie to follow.

As she watched, the girl turned and headed down the path leading to the cliffs, the wind plucked and played with her hair.

Kylie pounded on the window. "Stop! Come back."

But the child continued on, turning once to wave again, urging her to follow. The strength of the wind increased, blowing the child's hair back from her face.

Oh my God, it was Andrea! Andrea Greenley!

Frantic, Kylie ran for her coat. No time to waste. She needed to help Andrea. Needed to rescue her.

She yanked open the door and stepped out into the raging blizzard.

MICHAEL MOVED the cursor up to the menu bar and clicked on Quit. His latest article was almost done, but a quick glance at the clock told him that it was after 3:00 a.m. He'd stop for now and then do one last run through in the morning. Time enough to e-mail the finished product to his editor in the morning.

Stretching, he got up and walked over to the window. He had chosen a room on the second floor, on the west side of the hotel. Templer hadn't been happy, protesting that the suite was small and had no view, but Michael was only interested in the view overlooking Daniel McKee's tiny caretaker's cabin. He hadn't liked the fact that Kylie had decided to stay the night alone outside the walls of the main hotel.

He wasn't sure why he was worried about her, he just was. The thought of being able to lift the curtain and look down on the cabin had given him some peace of mind.

He pushed aside the drape with one finger and studied the courtyard below. Wind whipped snow up off the yard and dumped it onto the porch roof. The scene looked eerily reminiscent of one of his treks into Antarctica.

A flash of movement caught his eye.

"What the hell?"

He leaned closer to the window, using his breath and the palm of his hand to melt the frost clinging to the glass. A circle of smooth glass appeared.

He peered out into the blinding snow.

A woman stood in the clearing. Her hair, long, dark and whipped by the force of the wind, hid her face.

She wore a winter coat over a nightgown, but her legs were bare beneath the gown, the wind lifting the filmy material and whipping it about her exposed limbs.

Snow and ice danced in the stream of light coming from the spotlights at the back of the hotel. She stood in a whirlwind of swirling, twirling snowflakes.

Kylie?

What the hell was she doing outside in the snowstorm in the middle of the night? In a nightgown no less.

He pounded on the window to get her attention, but she couldn't hear him over the howl of the wind. She turned away and stood with her back to him, staring off toward the woods, as if waiting for someone to suddenly appear on the trail leading to the cliffs.

She was going to freeze out there.

Michael grabbed his jacket off the bed, shoved his feet into his boots and headed for the door.

He shoved against the back door, using his shoulder to wedge it open. A raging wind, fierce and relentless, slammed up against him as he stepped out onto the porch. Snow slipped down his boots from the drift lying up against the door.

He plowed through the drift to the steps and jumped off the porch. In the yard, the snow was up to his knees.

He shaded his eyes, trying to see. He could barely see Kylie; she still stood in the clearing, her back to him.

Hunching his shoulders, he slogged through the drifts, struggling to keep his balance.

At one point he stopped and cupped his hands, calling out, "Kylie!"

The wind snatched his words and sucked them into nothingness.

She didn't turn around, her frame small and vulnerable in the middle of the raging storm. The pines on either side of her whipped and dipped violently. She swayed, looking as though she might be snatched away at any moment.

He pushed harder through the drifts. He needed to get to her.

When he reached her, she turned, her expression confused.

"Where is she?" she shouted over the wind.

"Where's who?"

"The little girl."

Her body was shaking so hard she could barely speak.

"There's no one out here, Kylie." She swayed slightly and he reached down and picked her up, holding her close to his chest in a futile attempt to shelter her from the wind. "Come on, we need to get back to the cabin."

She didn't fight, all the energy seeming to drain out of her. He struggled through the snow, reaching the door and kicking it open. He leaned a shoulder against it, closing out the wind.

Crossing the room, he deposited her on the couch, yanking the blanket at one end up over her and tucked it around her legs and feet. She huddled deep within its warmth.

Turning, he grabbed a few logs out of the wood box and threw them on the dying embers. A few well placed jabs with the fire poker got the logs ignited. Heat started to pour out from behind the screen as he replaced it.

Her teeth chattered. "Th-thanks. Th-that f-feels wonderful."

He swung around and sat on the edge of the hearth, stretching his legs out in front of him. "What the hell were you thinking going out in the middle of a snowstorm in nothing but a nightgown and ski jacket? Are you insane?"

"Possibly."

"What does that mean?"

"It means that I think I might very well be crazy." She lifted her head, her eyes clouded with confusion. Fear. "I-I thought I saw someone out there."

"There was no one there but you."

She sat staring at him, mute.

He realized he'd shut her down and needed to get her talking again. "Who do you think you saw out there?"

She reached up and her fingers trembled slightly as she flipped several strands of wet hair back off her cheek. The confusion in her eyes intensified. She struggled to put what she was saying into words. "I-I saw someone. A child—a little girl. She was standing at the mouth of the path leading to the cliffs. She waved, wanted me to follow her."

She bent her head and scrubbed the bridge of her nose with the palm of her hand. It was an endearing gesture, one he remembered she'd used when he knew her eleven years ago, when she was confused or embarrassed.

As he watched, the muscles in her shoulders tightened. She obviously knew how her words sounded.

He got up and rounded the end of the coffee table. He pushed aside the blanket and sat on the edge of the couch. Reaching out, he took her hand. Her fingers were cold and trembled slightly in the warmth of his hand.

"No one was out there except us."

She looked up at him, her eyes filled with uncertainty. "I know you're right, but it doesn't change the fact that I saw something."

"Probably the spotlights and the snow. They played a trick on you—made you think you saw someone."

She shook her head. "I saw a child, Michael."

He touched the side of her face, his fingers sliding over smooth skin and silky hair as he pulled her forward. She didn't resist, but instead, leaned into him, her forehead touching his and then sliding over to rest on his shoulder.

He wrapped her in his arms, pressing her to him. The chill of her skin soaked through to his own body.

"No child would survive out there, Kylie. Besides, there aren't any children here at the lodge. And even if a child managed to ride a snowmobile out here from town, she wouldn't be out there at this time of the night."

"Then how do you explain what I saw?"

"What you saw was a trick of the light."

"It was the same girl I saw in the upstairs window when we arrived."

"Kylie—"

"I saw her, Michael. I *saw* her."

Her fingers slid beneath his jacket and tightened around him, digging into the thickness of his shirt. Her grasp was desperate, her gaze searching. And in that instant he hesitated, considering what she said.

Had she seen a child? Was he dismissing things too quickly simply because he didn't understand what was going on?

"It was Andrea Greenley," she whispered. "I—I think the girl I saw in the window was Andrea, too."

His hand, the one rubbing her upper back, stilled. He felt the frantic beat of her heart beneath his palm, the thud fast and furious, feeling as though it might pound right through her back.

He grasped her shoulders and leaned back to stare into her eyes. He could see her mentally bracing for his words of disbelief.

"Andrea is dead, Kylie. She died eleven years ago. You know that."

She jerked away from him, dragging the blanket with her as she huddled into the corner of the couch. She pulled her legs up to her chest and placed a wall of protection between them. Her fingers tightened on the blanket as she clutched it to her throat.

"*I saw her.* She called out to me and then started down the trail toward the cliffs."

He shook his head. "This is crazy. Andrea died from a fall."

She nodded, the motion sending a sheen of dark hair forward to shield the side of her face. "But I saw her. I know it was her."

"Look, you've been through a lot in the past few weeks—your father's death, returning to Cloudspin, finding a dead body. It's enough to send anyone over the edge."

"I'm not going over the edge."

"You're not making total sense, either. You're overtired. Stressed out."

She reached up and brushed back her hair. Her expression was pained. Haunted. "Thanks for your vote of confidence."

She shivered and pulled the blanket closer. She glanced away, her gaze settling on the flames snapping and crackling behind the grate. "I had a dream about her."

"A dream about who? Andrea?"

She nodded, her hair whispering against her cheek and neck. "It's a dream I've had more than once."

"Tell me about it."

She took a shuddering breath, a veil of uncertainty entering her eyes. Her indecision was blatant. He knew without her telling him that she was questioning whether or not to trust him.

In the end, she seemed to reach a decision, a willingness to share. For some reason that fact pleased him, and he wasn't sure why.

"It always starts off with me standing on the edge of the cliff overlooking the river." Her face was gaunt, her skin pale and paper thin. "You know how all of you used to jump off? How you'd take a running start and leap?"

He nodded, the memory of those exhilarating moments coming back in a sweet savage rush of adrenaline. They had all been a little crazy back then. Fearless. Unaware of the risks, defying death. Like all teens, they had thought they were invincible.

He couldn't help but wonder if his entire adult life up to this point hadn't been an attempt to reclaim that wondrous, boyish feeling of invincibility.

Across from him, Kylie sighed. Her eyes had a faraway look to them, as if she'd gone away for a moment, visiting the past in a way that she couldn't describe. He waited, unwilling to prod her for fear that she'd close down on him again.

Her eyelids fluttered and she was back. "I never told anyone, but I always wanted to make that jump. To leap out into space and drop down into the river. But I was too chicken. Too afraid. Sometimes I'd go up there alone and stand on the edge for hours, trying to get up enough courage to jump." Her fingers tightened into fists. "But I could never do it. I'd always back away, too scared to take a chance."

"Hell, Kylie, you were a kid. Only a few of us were able to make that jump, and we were all older than you. Besides, it was a crazy stunt to begin with. Any one of us could have been killed. You were the smart one. The one with the brains to realize it wasn't worth the risk."

"But I wanted to do it so badly and couldn't. I'd dream about doing it, even after I left Cloudspin. But then, a few years back, the dream changed. Suddenly I wasn't alone anymore when I stood on the cliff. I'd look down and see Andrea. She'd be hanging on to an outcropping of rocks, dangling there and crying for me to rescue her." Her voice broke and she swallowed hard. Her knuckles raked her upper thigh in frustration.

Michael reached out and gently touched her foot beneath the blanket, wrapping his fingers around her toes in an attempt to offer comfort.

She wet her lips with the tip of her tongue and continued, "In the dream, I always manage to reach down and grab her wrist." Her hands tightened in her lap as if she had actually latched on to something.

"Her wrist is frail, like a bird's wing, the bones tiny. I try to hang on, but I'm not strong enough. I can feel her slip."

Her voice trembled and he gently stroked the side of her leg. She seemed oblivious to his touch.

"I-in the dream, she cries out. Begs me not to drop her. But I can't hang on. She slips out of my grasp and falls."

A sob, deep and heartrending, ripped from her chest. He fought the urge to gather her to him, to comfort her. Something told him that if he moved, he'd disrupt the flow of the story and he knew she needed to get it out. Needed to tell it from start to finish.

"All I can see is her tumbling and falling in space. She cries out to me, screaming as she drops."

A shimmer of tears gathered along the rim of her eyes, threatening to fall. The deep brown of her eyes swam and died with the depth of her guilt.

"I—I try to jump in after her, but I can't." Her hands tightened even more, her knuckles turning white with anger. Desperation.

"Somehow, I can't summon the courage to jump. I see Andrea hit the water and then, she disappears beneath the water."

"Jeez, Kylie, how long have you been shoveling this load of guilt on yourself?"

She blinked. "What do you mean?"

"Hell, none of us could have saved Andrea. She wandered out to the cliffs before any of us even realized she was gone."

She dropped her head into her hands and her shoulders slumped. "But Gracie promised to watch her and I was hanging out with Gracie. She was our responsibility."

He shook his head. "As I remember it, Nikki was the one who was supposed to watch her."

Kylie raised her head and studied her hands. "But she asked Gracie to watch her. I promised to help."

"Don't you see that it's all in the past? What happened, happened. And to some degree all of us are responsible. You don't need to take the entire burden on yourself."

Kylie didn't look convinced. "Everything would have been fine if I hadn't been so eager to attend the party that night. Things would have been different if Gracie and I hadn't dragged Andrea along with us to the cliffs."

She swallowed hard. "But we desperately wanted to be part of the older crowd, and we weren't thinking straight. If we hadn't gone Andrea would be alive today."

"We were kids, Kylie. Kids make mistakes."

"Not mistakes like that."

She glanced up at him, her tears breaking free from their mooring and sliding unheeded from between her thick lashes. They made silvery trails down the center of her cheeks.

"Nothing you say will change anything," she whispered, her voice hoarse with emotion. "She was a little girl, only five years old. We should have protected her. She depended on us and we failed her."

"Dwelling on I should've or could've done this or that isn't going to bring her back. You've got to let this go."

She stood up and moved to the tiny kitchen area, her blanket trailing after her like a medieval cape.

She snatched up the teakettle sitting on the range, turned on the tap and filled it. Her motions were studied, controlled, as though if she didn't complete the task, she'd fall into a thousand tiny pieces.

When she was finished, she carefully set it on the burner and turned on the heat. He could see the muscle in her cheek clenching and unclenching as she fought the demons pressing in on her.

Leaning across the countertop, she pulled a metal canister to her and pried open the top. Her gaze met his across the room. "Only one packet of hot chocolate left. We'll have to share."

"Thanks, but I'd really rather have whiskey if you've got some."

She pointed to a cabinet next to the bookcase. "I think Dad kept some around for special occasions. Help yourself. I'm going to stick with the hot chocolate."

He got up and walked over to the cupboard. The liquor was right where she'd said it would be. He brought the bottle over to the couch. "Bring me a glass when you come back."

She reached into a cabinet and took down a glass, pausing a minute to trace her fingers over its surface. Her expression was pensive.

The teakettle whistled and she quickly poured hot water into a mug.

He watched her, struck by the sadness in her eyes. "What are you thinking?"

"I was remembering how many times I sat in this house, drinking Kool-Aid, munching on bologna sandwiches and giggling with Gracie." She jerked open a drawer and the silverware rattled. She grabbed a spoon, stuck it in the mug and stirred. "I should have kept in contact with her after the accident."

Her expression troubled, she set the mug and glass on a plastic tray and walked back over to the couch. "How bad was it for her after the accident?" She set the tray on the coffee table. "I mean, did her parents blame her for Andrea's death?"

She sat down, tucking her feet under her and held the mug with both hands. From the tightness of her grip, Michael knew she was trying to steady herself. To soak up the warmth of the hot liquid through the tips of her fingers.

He twisted off the cap on the whiskey and poured some in the glass. "She got the brunt of her parents' grief, especially her dad's. She kind of disappeared into a shell." He paused for a minute to consider what he'd said. "Come to think of it, I'm not entirely sure she ever came out of it. She never really seemed the same after the accident."

"What do you mean you think she got the brunt of her parents' grief?"

"She got sent away for a while."

"Sent away?"

He recapped the bottle and set it back on the table. "I heard rumors that she had a breakdown—got sent to a special school. I'm sure it was all very expensive and very discreet."

"I'm sorry I didn't try to keep in contact with her. She was a good friend. She didn't deserve to take all the blame." Her cheek, glowing with a pinkness that reassured him, rested on the back cushion as she sipped the cocoa.

"There was enough blame to go around, but Gracie definitely took on most of it. Things were never the same at Cloudspin after that." He lifted the glass and took a sip, the sting of the whiskey burning and heating his tongue as it slid down the back of his throat. "None of the others have ever been back until now."

He sat back, putting an arm up along the back of the couch, a few inches from the curve of her cheek resting on the cushion. He wanted to touch her skin, feel the glow that seemed to radiate off her, but he didn't want to push her. Didn't want to overwhelm her.

"You came back."

"The Adirondacks have always held a special pull for me. I can't explain it, but even though I've climbed all over the world, I keep coming back here. Keep looking for something."

"Do you know what it is? The specialness? The pull?"

He stretched his legs out in front of him, relaxing into the softness of the cushions, allowing her question to wash over him as the heat from the fire warmed him. "There's a magical quality that always seems to hover just out of my reach whenever I'm here. And I keep coming back, hoping that I'll discover how to capture it somehow."

He rolled his head to the left, allowing his gaze to connect with hers. Damn but she was beautiful. She had no idea how appealing she was. How open and vulnerable she seemed in the glow of the firelight spilling into the darkened room.

The depth and sincerity of her eyes sent something sharp and needy shooting through him. Something unexpected and not totally welcome. He didn't need this right now, not with the murder investigation heating up.

"Do you sometimes think about Andrea and the night she died?" Her voice was so soft that it was barely audible.

"Not as much as I used to. I told myself that I'd gotten closure on it. That I'd figured things out."

A stab of uncertainty caused him to pause for a moment. The weight of his own guilt regarding Andrea's death hovered black and uneven in one small corner of his mind, cut off for so many years and returning with a force that startled him.

Perhaps the headaches had a different meaning than he'd originally thought. Maybe they weren't connected to his fall. The uncertainty of that fact pressed in on him, filling him with a strange uneasiness. Uncertainty wasn't something he was used to. It wasn't in his nature.

Michael had always prided himself on his self-assurance. His certainty. These feelings were all new to him, and he wasn't liking them one bit.

"I'm beginning to think that maybe I didn't get the closure I thought I'd gotten," he said cautiously.

Her gaze lifted to meet his over the rim of her mug. The intensity of her eyes was stunning, breath stealing. "That bothers you a lot, doesn't it?"

"More than you know," he said.

She watched him, her eyes alive, the color rich and deep with awareness. The fire flickered, spilling pale light into the room, making her lips soften under its glow. He watched as they parted, and her breath, sweet and smelling of chocolate, whispered between them. Uneven. Slightly broken.

He leaned in and touched his mouth to hers. Just a brief brush. But as soon as he felt the smoothness, the sweet taste, he knew he wouldn't stop. He wrapped his hands around her upper arms and pulled her to him. The blanket slid off her narrow shoulders and pooled at her waist.

She sighed and her body pressed against his, the fine cotton of her nightshirt creating a thin shield between them.

Beneath his fingers, the muscles of her arms trembled

with anticipation. Somehow he knew without asking that she wouldn't resist. Wouldn't pull away.

His right hand slid beneath her arm to touch her rib cage, the beat of her heart strong and fast against the tips of his fingers. Her mouth opened beneath his, and he delved deeper, savoring the warmth of her mouth and quick dart of her tongue against his. Liquid silver.

He moved his hand upward, his thumb sliding over the underside of her firm breast to touch her nipple. Air hissed between her lips and she moaned softly.

She shifted and moved up and over him, one long, silky leg stealing across him, skimming his thighs and sending an uncontrollable heat surging through his lower belly. His hand reached down to brush aside the hem of her nightshirt, sliding beneath it to touch the softness of her inner thigh.

She seemed oblivious to her effect on him. But then, something told him that she knew exactly what she was doing. His thoughts scattered as she slowly lowered herself into his lap, fitting herself snugly against him. The rivet of his jeans rested against her most sensitive part.

She smiled, something secretive. Something so wild that it melted his insides to the consistency of hot molten lead. Heavy. Demanding.

Suddenly she was no longer vulnerable. Innocent. She was a woman who knew what she wanted, and the sharp release of need that slipped from between his lips elicited a deep, throaty laugh from within her.

Her hand came up to slide across his cheek to his ear, her fingers tangling in his hair. She dipped her head and her hair brushed the side of his face. She nipped his bottom lip with her teeth, watching his reaction through thick, slightly lowered lashes. Her eyes were smokey, filled with promise.

He was gone. Totally bewitched.

But as suddenly as it started, it stopped.

She pulled back, her breath coming in short ragged pants. When he moved forward, seeking to reclaim her, she stopped him, her palm flat against his chest. He could feel the pounding of his heart against the center of her hand, and he knew from the slight tightening of her fingers against the cloth of his shirt that she felt it, too.

Her eyelids opened, the smokiness and passion gone. "This doesn't feel right."

"I thought it felt just fine," he protested.

Before he could stop her, she slid off him and scooted across the cushion to the opposite corner of the couch. She drew her knees up to her chest, effectively and cleanly blocking him out.

"No, not fine." She shook her head and reached up to pull back the curls that a moment ago had caressed his skin with such vibrancy. She twisted them out of the way. "I'm sorry, but we both have too much going on in our lives right now to make a mistake like this."

"Who said it was a mistake?"

"Me." She lifted her head and those dark eyes sought out his. They were unflinching. Guilt-filled, beautiful and determined all at once. "And deep down, you know I'm right."

"I don't *know* that at all. All I know is that I like you. And I'm pretty sure you like me, too. What could possibly be wrong with that?"

"The timing's all wrong."

Frustration tugged at him. "Who the hell ever said timing had anything to do with how you feel about a person?"

She didn't respond but instead tightened her arms around her legs, reinforcing her resistance to him.

He stood up. "Hell and damnation, Kylie, timing is about numbers on a clock. It has nothing to do with how a person feels."

She shook her head, the set of her jaw firm, unflinching. "I disagree. We were caught up in the moment. A lot has happened in the past few hours, and I'm sure that none of the feelings we were just experiencing a few minutes ago has anything to do with reality."

"Felt pretty damn real to me."

She shrugged. "Believe me, you'll feel differently in the morning."

With a determination that even he couldn't miss, she stood up and pulled the blanket tighter around her. Even with her standing a few feet away, her posture practically screaming that she didn't want him near her, he could feel his body respond, shift into overdrive. But he fought it.

She looked so small and vulnerable standing in front of him, the firelight, warm and rosy, framing her in a reddish glow and softening the brilliance of her thick hair and the exotic tilt of her expressive eyes.

He fought the urge to overwhelm her, to lay her down on the thick braided rug and make every physical effort to change her mind. To make her scream his name and plead with him to never stop.

"You're sure this is what you want?" he asked.

She nodded, her lips pressed tightly together. "I'm positive."

"All right. I'll head back to the lodge." He paused. "You sure you're going to be okay?"

"I'll be fine."

But even he didn't miss the shadow of concern that slid across the surface of her eyes. She was still frightened, worried about what she'd seen earlier and the meaning of what had just happened.

But Michael knew from the rigid set of her shoulders that she would never allow him to step in and comfort her. He wasn't a fool. He knew why she was rejecting him, pushing him away. She saw him as dangerous. A possible killer.

And God help him, he couldn't be sure she wasn't right. After all, there was no denying that every woman he'd been intimately involved with over the past several months had ended up brutally murdered. There was no way he wanted Kylie to become the killer's next victim.

Chapter Seven

Kylie stepped out of the shower, grabbed a towel off the rack next to the sink and dried off. Steam rose off her body in tiny wisps. The cabin had cooled overnight, the fire dying.

After Michael had left around 4:30 a.m. she'd stacked more logs on the fire, rolled up in the blanket and pretended she might actually sleep.

But she hadn't.

Instead she'd laid there, her thoughts racing, running and colliding into each other until she was totally exhausted.

But no amount of analyzing and reanalyzing had given her a plausible reason for why she had allowed what happened to happen. Was she crazy? How could she have allowed him to kiss her? Worse yet, why had she allowed herself to respond?

Their timing was off, and Kylie was certain that the both of them weren't prepared to deal with the complications of any type of romantic entanglement. She had school to finish and a residency to start. Michael's life was even more complicated. He was in a virtual battle for freedom, if not his life.

Besides, she had no assurance that he wasn't somehow

mixed up in the murders. And something told her that even Michael wasn't certain about the part he played in the deaths of the women in Manhattan. Not to mention the maid here at Cloudspin.

She wiped the condensation off the window and peered outside. The storm still raged and overnight the snow had piled up with frightening speed. Two feet at least since she'd last looked. At this rate, they'd be buried beneath another two feet before noon.

Her gaze shifted to the clearing and the trail leading to the gorge. Nothing. Swirling snow but no child. Not even a sign of footprints in the snow. She dropped the curtain back in place.

She hadn't really expected to see anything. Michael had been right; her imagination, the shock of her father's death and her unexpected homecoming, had all conspired to make her see things. Guilt congealed in the pit of her stomach. She felt like a fool.

Turning away, she stepped back to the sink and stared into the mirror. Dark circles under her eyes practically shouted her lack of sleep.

"You're a damn fool," she said. The man had got her good. Rammed right through her defenses like they hadn't even existed. She couldn't afford to let it happen again.

Sighing, she grabbed the hair dryer and flicked it on, doing a quick blow dry.

A few dabs of make-up later, she studied her reflection. Not perfect but definitely an improvement. A little color to her cheeks and a decent job of covering up the dark circles beneath her eyes. It would have to do.

She yanked her robe off a hook on the back of the door. On either side of the mirror, the lights flickered twice and then went out.

"Great," she grumbled. "Hope I just blew a fuse."

She pulled on the robe and padded barefoot out into the kitchen. A quick check of the fuse box told her that the problem was much bigger.

She glanced out the window. The floodlights were off, too. She scanned the windows at the back of the hotel. They stared down at her, blank and dark. Apparently the storm had cut the electricity.

Her stomach growling, she did a quick inspection of the cupboards. Not much around. No coffee. No tea. Nothing but a few opened boxes of stale cereal and a loaf of what looked like petrified bread.

No way would she make it through a full day of packing without caffeine and something to eat. She'd have to dress and go up to the lodge. Maybe someone there would have word on when the electricity might get turned back on.

Ten minutes later, dressed in long underwear, worn jeans and a heavy wool sweater over a cotton turtleneck, Kylie shrugged into her jacket and slipped on her boots.

She had to look around for her mittens and hat, but decided the extra few minutes it took to locate them was well worth the effort. With the storm still raging outside, even the short walk up to the lodge could be dangerous. The thermometer hanging outside the kitchen window read a mind-numbing ten degrees.

Zipping up her jacket, she headed out the door and slogged through the snowdrifts covering the path to the hotel. The wind, fierce and bitter, changed directions, alternately pushing and pulling at her, making her trek seem impossibly long.

Gasping for breath, she scrambled up the back steps, stumbling and catching herself from falling several times. Someone needed to get out with a shovel and clear things off before she ended up killing herself. She made a mental note to tackle that job after she ate.

She pushed open the back door and practically fell onto the sparkling tile floor of the huge kitchen. She used the weight of her body to close the door, leaning against it for a moment to catch her breath.

"Wind seems to be picking up," a voice said behind her.

Kylie turned to see Sara Dell, the lodge's elderly cook standing in the middle of the kitchen. Her arms were crossed over her ample chest and a floured apron stretched across her oversized, lumpy body.

She smiled at Kylie and her lips, lined with age, turned up at the corners. A sense of relief spread through Kylie's chilled body at the sight of the woman. The smile was familiar, welcome.

Sara had served as the head cook at Cloudspin for what seemed like forever. She was a permanent fixture, her cooking talents legendary among the guests.

"Sara!"

Sara held up a hand and pointed at her feet. "First the boots. Don't be tracking any of that nasty snow onto my clean floor."

Kylie grinned and bent down to yank off her boots. She set them on the boot tray and then ran the length of the kitchen into the elderly cook's embrace.

"How ya doing, sugar baby?" Sara asked, her arms closing around her and trapped her against her softly padded body. "I've missed your sweet face around this old place. Thought I'd never get to see you again."

Kylie inhaled the smell of butter, minced garlic and sweet red wine. The scent was imbedded in the old woman's clothing, in her skin. For Kylie, it held comforting memories.

Memories of afternoons spent sitting at the huge oak kitchen table, her legs swinging and hitting the rungs of the ladder back chairs and downing frothy glasses of ice-cold milk followed by chewy oatmeal cookies sprinkled liberally with fat, sun-sweetened raisins.

Sara was a fifth generation North Country woman, and she never bought into the idea of cookies and milk spoiling a child's appetite. According to Sara, they were a staple of every child's diet, appropriate at any time of the day. All the children who had spent any time at Cloudspin knew Sara's philosophy regarding cookies and they all took advantage of it.

When the hug ended, Sara stepped back, her eyes searching Kylie's as she clucked her tongue in disapproval. "Entirely too thin. Hope you haven't turned into one of those skinny city girls I see all the time in the magazines. I always thought you were smarter than that." She shook her head. "'Course that just means that I'll have to fatten you up for the short time you're here."

With a grin, Kylie sniffed the air. "Hope you weren't saying that as a means of punishment because I can feel the pounds packing on just inhaling whatever it is you're cooking."

"Pancakes with wild blueberry compote and real Vermont maple syrup. Add a few links of my homemade sausages to sweeten the deal and you're on your way. Might have made something a bit more elegant for your homecoming, but the storm put out the electricity."

"I noticed the power outage. Lucky for me I was able to get my hair dry before it went out." Kylie frowned. "How can you cook with the electricity out?"

"My woodstove." Sara nodded in the direction of a huge cast-iron monstrosity sitting in the far corner of the kitchen. "Your daddy was always talking about taking it out to the dump and putting it out of its misery. But I wouldn't let him. Told him that the darn thing would come in handy one day. Today appears to be that day."

Sadness clouded her eyes and she reached up and patted Kylie's cheek. "I'm so sorry about your daddy's passing. We're going to miss him around here. Especially me."

Kylie laid her hand over the older woman's. "I know, Sara. He would never stop talking about you when he came to visit. I'd serve him cold cereal for breakfast and he'd moan and groan about how he couldn't wait to get back to Cloudspin and your cooking."

"Men," the old woman sniffed. "All they can think about is their stomachs. That daddy of yours was the ultimate eating machine. A bottomless pit, if you ask me. I couldn't keep his fingers out of anything I made."

Then she laughed. "Now don't you be telling the health department that I allow such behavior in my kitchen. Truth be known, I swatted that man's hands with a wooden spoon more times than I'd care to count."

"What time did the police finish up last night?" Kylie asked, shifting gears.

"Mr. Templer told me they left around 2:00 a.m. Said

they'd be back today, but I'm guessing that with the storm as bad as it is they won't be pulling in here anytime soon."

She reached into the pocket of her worn cotton apron and pulled out a linen handkerchief with lace edging. She swiped the bottom of her heavily veined nose. "Sorry I wasn't here to greet you when you got in last night. I've been fighting a bad cold and stayed in my cabin, sleeping all day. Never even knew about all the commotion until I came to the main lodge this morning."

Before Kylie could inquire about how she was feeling, Sara turned and headed back toward the stove. She grabbed an old-fashioned spatula sitting on the top and used it to flip one of the oversize pancakes sizzling on the grill.

Kylie went to the table and picked up the heavy crystal pitcher of orange juice sitting in the center. She poured herself a glass and sipped.

"I heard about Molly." Sara shook her head. "Poor, sweet girl stopped in to check on me before she went out to get those houses ready for guests. Can't believe she's gone."

Startled, Kylie set her orange juice down. "Any chance you remember what time it was when Molly stopped by to check on you?"

Sara popped two pancakes onto the warming rack. "Of course I do. I was watching Judge Judy." She grinned over her shoulder at Kylie. "I love that woman. She don't take no guff from anyone. Speaks her mind like plain folk do. The show had already started by the time Molly stopped by."

Kylie's heart sped up, but before she could comment, Sara turned toward her, waving her spatula for emphasis. "You should have seen the show. Some trashy mouthed seventeen-year-old girl was suing her mama for lack of financial support. Little hussy moved in with her no-good boyfriend and thought her poor mom should support her lazy butt. Probably wanted her to take care of that no-good, beer-swigging boyfriend of hers, too."

Sara turned back to the stove and loosened the edges of one of the pancakes. "But Judge Judy set that girl straight. Told her that she needed to grow up and get a life. I'm guessing from Judge Judy's expression that she wanted to paddle that spoiled girl's behind within an inch of her life."

She waved the spatula through the air again. "I would have gladly done it for her if I'd been there."

Kylie swallowed her impatience. "Do you remember *exactly* what time Molly came over? What time she left?"

Sara paused, her expression puzzled. "What's wrong, honey bun? You sound upset."

"I just need to know if you remember the *exact* time that Molly came to visit."

"Whatever for?"

"Because Ms. McKee is desperately looking for an alibi for her good friend Michael Emerson," a new voice chimed in.

Kylie swung around to find Detective Denner standing in the doorway. Apparently he hadn't left last night with the others. Not that it surprised her. He didn't seem like the kind who was about to let Michael out of his sight.

Denner sauntered in, letting the heavy door swing shut behind him. He reached out and snatched a MacIntosh from a clay bowl on the counter. "Got a paring knife?"

"In the drawer to the left," Sara said, her eyes narrowing.

Kylie could tell from the quick look the cook had shot in her direction that she'd picked up on her resentment of

Denner's intrusion. Sara wasn't a slouch when it came to reading people, she'd had plenty of practice working at the lodge, and Kylie was fairly certain the old cook would give the New York City detective more than he bargained for if he tried any of his bullying tactics on her. Sara was more than a match for him.

"Guest or no guest, I don't like my kitchen messed up. March yourself over and get a plate, mister."

Denner studied the elderly cook for a moment and then nodded. He grabbed a plate off the sideboard and sat at the table. His big hands sliced the blade into the apple and leveraged off a hunk. He lifted the slice to his mouth, balancing the section on the shiny metal.

He paused, the slice halfway to his mouth. "Can't bite into apples anymore. Dentures. Happens when you get old."

Sara sniffed. "Not if you take care of your teeth, it doesn't. You lookin' for breakfast?"

"Like Ms. McKee, I'm anxious to hear what time Ms. Jubert arrived in your room yesterday. And the time she left." He grinned, no warmth reaching his eyes. "But I wouldn't mind a stack of those pancakes, either."

Sara stacked four of the golden pancakes onto a dish, drizzled a generous amount of the warm syrup over them and speared four sizzling sausage links. Walking over to the table, she deposited them in front of the detective. "You want coffee with that?"

"That would be nice." Denner tucked a napkin on his lap and glanced at Kylie. "Care to join me?"

In spite of the hunger rumbling in the pit of her belly, Kylie shook her head. She had no desire to sit at the same table as the man who had tried so hard to intimidate her last night. And from the looks of things, he hadn't undergone any major attitude adjustments since she'd last seen him.

She said, "Orange juice is fine for now."

He shrugged, the squint of his eyes telling her that her discomfort seemed to amuse him. "Suit yourself."

He glanced back at Sara. "So, about those times."

"Molly got to my room around 4:10. I had just taken some medicine and she'd brought me a tray with green tea and honey. We shared a cup before she left around 5:00 to start work on preparing the Greenley residence."

Denner frowned; he didn't like her answer. "Are you sure she didn't get there earlier?"

Sara picked up the ladle and scooped up more batter, pouring the thick mixture onto the hot griddle. "I wouldn't have said what I said unless I was sure."

Relief bubbled up inside Kylie. If Molly was alive at 4:30 yesterday, there was no way that Michael was responsible for her death. He was with her from 4:30 until they arrived at the lodge together. They'd been in each others' company until they'd gone up to the fourth floor and found Molly. He was in the clear.

Denner seemed to sense her relief and his expression went decidedly sour. He used his fork to tear off a hunk of pancake and shoved it into the corner of his mouth. He chewed, staring off into space.

"Maybe the coroner needs to revisit his estimate of the time of death," he said finally.

"Her body was still warm when I tried CPR," Kylie said. "With the low temperature in the upstairs rooms, there's no way that Molly's body would still be warm unless she died a short time before we arrived. And that makes it impossible for Michael to have killed her, skied ten miles out on the access road and met me. No one, not even an Olympic-caliber skier, could have skied that distance in the time required by your scenario."

"Maybe he killed her, took off in his car, parked it somewhere and then pretended to be out skiing. You're a useful alibi. He's smart enough to know that."

"Did the police find a car nearby?"

"Hard to say in this weather. But it's a possibility we'll have to investigate before all is said and done."

"But your theory of what happened isn't so pat now, is it?"

Denner shoveled in another bite. "No theory is ever pat, Ms. McKee. It's a jigsaw puzzle and I'm the puzzle master. I'll figure it out."

"I just hope you're not so set on the conclusion you're looking for that you miss an important clue."

Denner smiled. "Still set on being his champion, aren't you."

Kylie set her glass in the stainless-steel sink and headed for the door leading to the hall. "I'm no one's champion, Detective Denner. I'm only interested in seeing that an overzealous cop doesn't railroad a friend of mine."

She nodded to Sara and slipped out the door. Behind her, Kylie heard Denner's grating laugh. And as the door swung shut, he calmly requested seconds on pancakes.

KYLIE'S STOCKING feet hit the hardwood floors of the darkened hall with a satisfying smack. Pain radiated up through the soles of her feet.

Anger regarding the police detective's one-track mind ripped up along the ridge of her spine. The man was like a dog worrying a meatless bone. Something told her that he was the type of guy who would tear and gnaw on things until he got them to fit his picture of how things should be. It didn't bode well for Michael.

She cut through the shadowy, dark dining room and entered the main lobby. This room was empty, too. Apparently everyone else had decided to sleep in.

She swung through the archway and walked down the hall leading to the library. The light from the bank of windows along the outer wall was faint, the lack of sun leaving the narrow corridor shrouded in an oppressive darkness that seemed to reflect everyone's mood.

Dust motes drifted lazily in the air and a relentless chill sunk down through the wool of her sweater. If they didn't get the heat turned on soon, ice would start to form on the windows. They'd all be in trouble if that happened since conserving body heat would be next to impossible once the outside chill totally took over the interior of the lodge.

She pushed open the library door and stepped inside. A quick sniff sent the smell of old books, cedar and wood smoke rushing up her nose. Comforting.

Someone had lit four storm candles and left them standing on a heavy platter in the center of the coffee table. Their flames jumped and flickered in the draft from the open door. Behind the elaborate scrolled fireplace grate, a fire crackled cheerfully in the gloom. The chill from the hall was less intense in here.

Apparently Templer had instructed his staff to keep a fire going in all the public rooms in an attempt to keep the plunging indoor temperatures from overwhelming them.

She closed the door. Better to keep the warm air inside.

From across the room, the heart stone in the center of the mantel glowed a warm welcome.

Kylie knew the reason she was drawn to the room. It was the stone, it brought her comfort, a feeling that her father was closer somehow.

She crossed the room and stood in front of the hearth, reaching out to lightly trace the outline of the heart. Her fingertips tingled as her dad's voice echoed in her head, telling her how the stone would always be the center of the fireplace, a memento of the time they'd spent together rebuilding the hearth.

To the far right of the hearth, sitting on a canvas drop cloth, along with several bags of mortar, were piles of loose sandstone. Apparently her dad had been preparing for some renovations. Upkeep on the lodge's aging interior was a constant battle, one her father waged during the slow winter months.

She moved over to stand near the drop cloth. Before he'd died, her dad had started the sorting process, putting similarly colored and sized stones in piles.

She reached down and picked up a stone. It was heavy, the edges rough and gritty but the center smooth and silky with a kaleidoscope of muted earth colors.

"What are you up to?"

She jumped, almost dropping the stone on her foot. She turned to see Michael standing a few feet away. The man was like some kind of wild, exotic polecat the way he managed to get around without making a sound.

He was dressed differently than last night. Gone were the tight ski pants and in their place worn jeans hugged his lean, muscular legs. A thermal shirt peeked out from beneath a blue plaid flannel shirt, the color enhancing the rich tan of his skin. How was it that wealthy people always managed to look tan? She knew she looked like a pale ghost next to him.

His boots, dinged and scuffed from use, completed the picture. Rugged and nice. Way too nice.

Her mouth went dry and she reminded herself that she'd already decided that they weren't ready for any kind of relationship. Too bad her body wasn't in the mood to listen.

"I'm getting the distinct feeling I need to hang a bell around your neck just so I know when you enter a room," she said with a touch of irritation.

He rounded the end of the couch and took up a position a few inches away. The sharp scent of soap, pine and man hit her hard.

Her hands tightened around the edges of the rock. If there was one thing Kylie knew it was there was nothing worse for a woman's out of control libido than a clean-smelling, sexy man with hair that curled and hugged the collar of his shirt. It was slightly tousled as if he'd been out in the wind.

If she didn't watch out, their attraction could get out of hand, just as it had last night.

"Sorry, didn't mean to startle you. But you were so engrossed in studying that pile of rocks that a herd of elephants could have charged through here and you wouldn't have blinked an eye." He pointed at the stone in her hands. "You planning on chucking that at me or did you have something else in mind?"

"You thinking you deserve a good stoning?"

One corner of his mouth twisted with amusement before he got serious. "I'm thinking that maybe I took advantage last night and that I need to apologize."

His voice was low and smooth, and she felt those same feelings she'd fought last night start to stir with a fierceness that was frightening. Damn, but this man had the ability to get under her skin.

She shrugged with more nonchalance than she'd thought possible considering the condition of her insides. "You didn't do anything I hadn't been thinking about all on my own."

That and a few other possibilities, she admitted to herself. "But I'm guessing that we'd both be better off forgetting about last night."

"Hard to do," he said.

Her belly turned to liquid fire, but she ignored it and turned away, nodding toward the stack of stones her father had laid out before he died. "I was doing a little reminiscing. Thinking on all those afternoons I used to help my dad keep these old fireplaces in tip-top condition. He was a true artist."

"He was. His legacy is the condition of this old place."

She smiled, appreciating his tribute to a man who had spent a lifetime in the service of the old lodge.

She leaned down and placed the reddish stone shot through with ochre streaks on the stack her dad had already started. It slipped seamlessly into place. A perfect fit, as if it was meant to go there. A warmth washed over her. She hadn't lost her touch. Her eye for size and color was something she'd inherited from her dad.

She returned to the pile of stones in the corner and selected another one, this one bigger, bulkier. As she bent down to grab it, she grunted under the weight of it.

She felt Michael move behind her before she actually saw him. A flash of something warm and liquidy rushed through her as his body pressed in on her. The firm muscles of his outer thigh brushed her right hip as he leaned in to place his hands over hers, lifting the stone effortlessly.

She snatched her hands out from beneath his calloused palms and stepped back. "Your hands are cold."

"Sorry, I was up early and decided to go out and check things. I shoveled off the front porch and then skied over to my house to make sure everything was all right."

He shifted the weight of the stone closer to his body, cradling it in his big hands with ease. "With the electricity off, I'm probably going to have some damage from burst pipes."

He moved over to the hearth. "Where do you want it?"

"On top of those two right there." She pointed. "No, a little to the right. That's it, there."

He dropped the stone into place and stepped back. She moved around him to jiggle the rock slightly, repositioning it. She tried without much success to ignore the current of heat that shot through her as she brushed up against him again. The man was a damn furnace with all the heat he generated.

"I saw Denner in the kitchen a few minutes ago. Sara Dell saw Molly alive around 4:40 yesterday. That makes it impossible for you to have killed her."

"Bet that got Denner's shorts in a knot."

Kylie laughed at the mental image. "He wasn't real happy."

"He'll find a way to twist it." Michael moved back over to the drop cloth to examine the other rocks. Kylie knew without him saying anything that he was putting space between them. She wondered if he was fighting the same feelings she was.

"Sara isn't the type to be pushed around by anyone," she said.

"No, she isn't. Thanks for letting me know what she said. I have a feeling that Denner would never tell me. He isn't about to let me off the hook anytime soon."

Before Kylie could respond, the library door swung open and Gracie burst into the room. Her face was taut, jittery.

Michael handed Kylie the rock he'd been turning over in his hands and straightened up. "What's up, Gracie? You look a little scattered."

"Have you seen Heather?" Her voice was tense, her cheeks flushed.

Michael shook his head and glanced at Kylie. "Have you seen her?"

"Not since last night."

She set the stone on the hearth and stood up, brushing her hands together to get the rock dust off.

From her spot near the door, Gracie chewed the side of her cheek. "When I got up this morning, I stopped by Heather's room. She said last night that she wanted to eat breakfast with me. She wasn't there. Her room was empty."

"Maybe she got up early and went down on her own. No big deal." He grinned and nodded toward the window. "No one is going anywhere in this weather. Did you check the kitchen? Sara's serving breakfast in there because it's warmer than the main dinning room."

"I've checked everywhere." Gracie rubbed her hands together, the tenseness in her voice going up a notch. "It's not like her to take off without telling anyone." She glanced toward the windows, her eyes seeming to register the menacing nature of the storm lashing the glass. "You're sure she wouldn't go outside? I mean her jacket's gone and so are her boots."

"She was probably just cold and put on her jacket and warm boots to keep the chill off," Michael said. "Even with the fires going these rooms are pretty damp. Maintenance is working on getting the generator up and running, but I wouldn't hold my breath."

Behind Gracie, the door swung open again and her sister, Nikki, walked in. The place was getting to be a regular Grand Central Station and it was beginning to bug Kylie. She had hoped to have a few hours alone to get her thoughts together; now she was surrounded.

"Are you still angsting about Heather?" Nikki demanded. "You've been up since five o'clock worrying about her. Relax. She's around here somewhere."

A sheepish expression crossed Gracie's face, but then she straightened up, bracing her shoulders as if she needed reinforcements to deal with her sister. "I'm worried about her. What if she decided to go out? She said she wanted out of here last night."

"No chance of that happening. Heather's a wimp," Nikki said. "I had to twist her arm to even consider coming up here this weekend. She made it perfectly clear that she planned on nailing down a spot at the bar and staying there while we all went out and made fools of ourselves on skis."

Gracie moved to the windows, pushed aside the drape and stared out. "Then where is she? There aren't that many rooms open. The maintenance men have closed everything off except the main floor and the second floor. Heather wouldn't just wander off exploring. She's scared to death of this place. Freaked out by the murder."

"As were we all," Nikki retorted, moving to plop down on the couch. She didn't look too freaked out, but then Kylie couldn't be sure it wasn't an act.

"None of us were as bothered about it as Heather." Gracie glanced at Kylie, her eyes filled with guilt. "She stopped by my room last night. Wanted to know if I'd let her sleep in my room. She was afraid to be alone. But I'm a lousy sleeper and I told her that she'd be fine in her own room. I should have let her stay."

Kylie walked over and wrapped an arm around her friend's shoulders. "It's okay, Gracie. We'll find her. Everything's going to be fine."

Michael headed for the door. "Let's get everyone into the kitchen and decide how we're going to search for her. She's got to be around here somewhere."

Within a few minutes, they had assembled the other guests—Craig Templer, Detective Denner and the few remaining members of the staff not working on the generator—in the warm, open area of Sara's kitchen.

Michael took charge. "I think that we should divide up into teams of three and search the lodge for Heather. She hasn't been here in a while and she might have gotten disoriented."

"All she'd have to do is give a yell and one of us would hear her," one of the waiters said.

"We didn't hear Molly up on the fourth floor," Gracie reminded him. "None of us heard anything when she was killed."

"True…" the waiter said, his voice trailing off.

"Where have you been all morning, Emerson?" Denner asked, the accusation in his voice obvious.

"He's been with me in the library," Kylie stated.

"Always his protector, huh, Ms. McKee?" Denner said with a knowing smile.

Kylie didn't bother to respond. There wasn't any point. The man had already made up his mind that Michael was somehow involved. Nothing, not even Sara's statement earlier had changed a thing.

Before anyone could speak, the back door swung open and the two maintenance men from last night trooped in. Snow and an icy wind blew in through the open door. They stomped their feet and shook loose snow off their heavy jackets like two oversize St. Bernards. Bending down, they removed their boots before Sara could remind them.

"Well, did you get it running?" Sara asked.

"Sure hope so," the beefy maintenance man from last night said. "Try the lights."

Sara flicked the switch, and lights flooded the warm kitchen, chasing away the gloominess that seemed to creep out of the dark corners.

"Saints be praised!" Sara grabbed two mugs off the counter and swung around to scoop up the coffeepot sitting on the wood burning stove. She poured dark, aromatic coffee into the mugs. "Sit down and I'll serve you up a well-deserved breakfast. You must be freezing."

Neither man argued. They shrugged out of their jackets and quickly seated themselves at the huge plank farm table.

"Did you see anyone outside, Tommy?" Templer asked.

Blowing on his steaming coffee the heavy-set maintenance man glanced around, realizing for the first time that all the occupants of the lodge were congregated in the kitchen. He looked mildly surprised.

"Saw two people out skiing earlier. Shouted at them that they were damn fools to be out in this weather. But they didn't seem in the mood to listen. Kept right on going."

Gracie stepped closer to the man, her face lined with concern. "Was one of them wearing a pink parka?"

Tommy frowned. "Yeah, come to think of it, one of them did have on some kind of puffy pink jacket. Damn thing didn't look sturdy enough to ward off the cold blowing out there. But you city folk aren't interested in me commenting on what you wear, right?" He leaned across the table, grabbed the spoon out of the sugar bowl and dumped two heaping spoonfuls into his coffee. He took another sip and smacked his lips. "Good coffee, Sara."

"Did you see what direction they went?" Michael asked.

"Looked like they were headed out toward the cliffs." Tommy shook his head. "Can't understand people taking a risk like that. This is not the kind of day to be out fooling around."

"What was the other person wearing?" Denner asked.

Tommy shrugged and glanced at his partner. "You remember, Del?"

Del shook his head. "Sorry, I was concentrating on getting the generator shed door open. The damn lock was frozen solid."

Tommy glanced up at the rest of them. "Can't be sure but I think the person was dressed in black pants and jacket. Looked a little better bundled up than the gal in the pink getup."

"All right, some of us need to concentrate on searching the lodge. The rest of us can ski out to the cliffs to see if anyone is out there," Michael said.

Kylie glanced toward the windows, noting the fierceness of the storm. If possible, things looked worse than when she had trudged over to the lodge a few hours ago.

"No one could last out there more than a few minutes," Nikki stated. "There's no way Heather would take that chance."

"Hopefully you're right," Michael said. "But if Heather isn't here in the hotel, where is she?"

No one had any suggestions. The silence in the kitchen was heavy.

Finally Sara spoke up, "You're not saying that someone took off with her and then ditched her somewhere out in that mess, are you?"

"I'm not saying anything. We don't know what happened, but we need to check out all possibilities. And since the last time someone who looked like her was spotted headed out to the cliffs, we need to check things out."

"Sounds like you're speaking from the position of knowledge, Emerson," Denner said.

"As hard as you're going to find this to believe, Detective, I haven't seen Heather since last night."

Kylie looked at him, acutely aware that he'd admitted less than an hour ago that he'd gone out skiing. Was it possible that he was the other person the maintenance men had seen? He'd been wearing black ski clothes last night when she'd met him on the access road.

A renewed stab of fear shot through her. Even she had to admit that it might be too much of a coincidence.

"I'll change and go see if I can find her." He moved toward the door.

"Hold it, Emerson," Denner ordered. "No way in hell am I letting you out of my sight."

Michael paused, his gaze cool and appraising. "Then we have a big problem, Detective. If there is any chance Heather is out there, I don't intend to let her face the elements alone. But you are certainly welcome to come along."

He smiled without a trace of humor. "Of course, the trail is pretty rough going, so you'd better be prepared to keep up."

Denner frowned. "I don't know how to ski."

"Well, then you have a problem, don't you? Especially since I'm not in the mood to drag your sorry butt down the trail on my back."

"How do I know you won't take off?" Denner pressed.

"Because I'm giving you my word that I'll be back." Michael glanced around the kitchen, his gaze settling on his friend, "As added insurance, I'll take Steven with me. He can make sure I come back."

"Oh, joy," Steven muttered under his breath.

Michael shot him an apologetic shrug, then pushed open the door to the dining room. He paused, seeming to consider something.

Finally, he turned toward Kylie. She knew without him even speaking what was coming.

"I'd like you to come along too, Kylie. Heather might need your medical expertise." There was a touch of apology in his voice, as if he realized he was asking a lot.

She nodded, agreeing to his request. At least she wouldn't be alone with him.

Michael's gaze shifted to Nikki. "Find some ski clothes for Kylie. Make sure she's well protected."

Nikki brushed past her. "Fine. But you're not going without me. I'm coming too."

Michael didn't waste any time looking surprised or trying to convince her otherwise. "We can always use the extra pair of hands."

He glanced at Denner, his expression amused. "Besides, I'm sure Detective Denner is pleased that another pair of eyes will be watching to see that I don't take off for parts unknown."

The expression on Michael's face startled Kylie. He looked entirely too happy, almost elated. The euphoric glint in his eye told her that he was relishing the thought of venturing out in the storm.

No doubt his famous adrenaline-junkie side had kicked in. Somehow she couldn't muster the same enthusiasm. Not by a long shot.

"Come on, I've got some extra ski clothes in my luggage," Nikki said.

Her brusque tones spoke to the level of resentment she felt regarding Kylie's participation in the skiing expedition. Inwardly Kylie shrugged off the bad vibes. Too bad. She was going.

Bracing her shoulders, Kylie followed Nikki out the door as a strange sense of foreboding niggled at the back of her neck. The fact that Heather was gone, vanished without a trace, had reawakened her feelings of suspicion. Fear pressed in on her.

Leaving the lodge and venturing out to the cliffs felt wrong. Devastatingly wrong. But somehow, they'd been drawn to make the trip to the very place that had changed their lives eleven years ago.

The past called loudly.

Too loudly to ignore.

Chapter Eight

Gusts of wind created whirlwinds of snow that swirled and twisted around their bodies as they headed for the cliffs. Their skis cut through the drifts cleanly, but the terrain was rough and uneven. It made for slow going.

Overhead, the sky hung low. So low Kylie felt like she could reach up and brush her fingers along the underside of one of the clouds. They were vile-looking clouds, thick and gray and edged in a threatening black.

On all sides, the pine trees whipped in the wind and groaned under the weight of the snow clinging to their branches. Lush green bowed beneath white, the branches touching the ground and signaling their surrender.

But the storm wasn't backing down, it raged on. No mercy for anything or anyone.

Kylie tucked her chin to her chest, desperate to capture some of the warmth protecting her torso beneath the heavy storm jacket. Goggles kept the snow out of her eyes, but the ski mask Nikki had given her provided only limited protection. Frozen particles hit the openings made for her eyes, nose and mouth, stinging her face.

She was cold. So cold she realized she hadn't felt the

tips of her fingers since they'd left the lodge a few minutes ago. The thermometer outside the ski shed had registered ten below. Too cold for anyone to be outside.

The rope around her waist tugged and pulled at her, reminding her to keep moving. She dug in her poles and settled into a jerky rhythm.

She was out of practice after years of living in the city. Cross-country skiing in Central Park was a far cry from skiing on terrain like this, and the weather conditions only made things worse.

Before they'd left the shed, Michael had tied them all together with a length of nylon climbing rope. He'd patiently explained that it was an added precaution to keep them from wandering off the trail. The idea had merit since Kylie couldn't see two feet in front of her.

But she couldn't help but wonder what would happen if Michael lost *his* way? They could wander around in circles for hours. Or worse, they could ski off the edge into the gorge.

She shuddered beneath the weight of her jacket and tried shaking off the thought. No need to scare herself more than she already was.

Up ahead, almost hidden in the swirling snow, she could make out the vague outline of Michael. He was poling against the wind, his powerful body concentrating on breaking a trail for the rest of them.

Directly behind her, the rope stretching out like a nylon umbilical cord, was Nikki. Steven brought up the rear. Each of them had a good-size backpack strapped to their bodies.

Her own contained a well-stocked emergency first-aid kit Sara kept in the kitchen. The other packs carried water, hot tea, power bars and an assortment of climbing gear.

Steven towed a red plastic sled, a toy kept expressly for the kids who visited the lodge. Blankets were strapped inside. Kylie knew Michael had considered the possibility that if Heather was found, she might not be able to walk, due to injury or frostbite.

A gust of wind hit her hard, and Kylie realized the direction had shifted again. The chilling blast was now coming out of the north. She inhaled cold air and dug her poles in harder, lengthening her stride to keep up.

Ahead, Michael stopped and then moved quickly toward a cluster of pines hugging the side of the trail. Through a heavy veil of snow, she watched him lean down and pluck something dark off one of the tree limbs.

She squinted against the flakes hitting her goggles, trying to see what he'd found. But before she reached him, he stuffed whatever it was into the pocket of his jacket.

She slid to a stop next to him.

"We're almost to the cliffs." He reached out to steady her. She welcomed the strength of his fingers as they sunk down through the cloth of her coat, imparting his confidence.

"You okay?" he asked.

She nodded, unable to speak due to the force of the wind and the fact that she was more than a little winded. He moved closer, shielding her from the wind with his height and bulk. It took all her willpower not to lean against him and rest.

"What did you find?" she asked.

He hesitated but then stuck his hand in his jacket and

pulled out a black ski cap. The gold logo on the front stared up at her. It was the same hat he'd worn the night she'd almost run him over.

A heaviness settled into her shoulders. There was only one way that hat could have gotten out here. Bitterness and fear filled her throat and she couldn't meet his eyes.

"I know what you're thinking, but I swear to you, I haven't been out here." The wind snatched and pulled at his words, sending them tumbling away.

Numb, she nodded.

He shifted closer and reached up to tuck a gloved hand under her chin. He tried to force her to look up, but she turned her head away, her thoughts racing. She'd been a fool to believe him. Denner had been right. She needed to return to the lodge.

"Look at me, Kylie." He ripped off his goggles.

Reluctant, a terrible dread pulling at her, she forced herself to look into his eyes.

Clear blue serenity touched her. There was no missing the pull, the request for trust.

"Then how did the hat get here?"

"I don't know. But I haven't been out on this trail."

"It didn't get out here on its own, Michael."

"I realize that. I'm as stumped as you are."

Strangely enough, she felt her own fear start to dissipate, to melt under the warmth of his gaze.

She desperately wanted to believe him. He held their lives in his hands.

"Someone is setting me up to take another fall. I don't know why, but I intend to find out."

She watched as he shoved the cap back in his pocket.

She couldn't help but wonder if he'd make its existence known to Denner when they got back to the lodge.

Kylie glanced over her shoulder, checking on the progress of the others. Steven had moved up next to Nikki and was bent down, checking her left binding. Nikki signaled they were all right.

Kylie shivered as the wind howled around them. "I don't understand why Heather would come out here. It doesn't make any sense."

Michael bent his head, bringing his lips close to her ear. She felt the flat of his hand against the small of her back, as if he was steadying her, drawing her closer.

"I agree. None of this makes any sense. All I can think is that maybe she got frightened. The murder of the maid spooked her and someone—whoever brought her out here—tricked her into believing that he'd get her back to town."

"But according to Nikki, Heather can't ski. I'm a fairly decent cross-country skier and I'm struggling. What would have made her believe that she could ski out?"

"Good question." She heard the puzzlement in his voice. "Fear can be a pretty good motivator."

She nodded. He wasn't wrong in that department.

"The storm has gotten worse in the last hour or so." He bent his head again, brushing up against her. She felt the warmth and moistness of his breath against the side of her face. "Conditions might have been better when the two of them started out."

"Maybe, but people don't typically take off in the middle of a blizzard."

"People who know better don't. But Heather's a city gal. She might not have really understood how dangerous the conditions were. Whoever convinced her to come was someone she trusted."

Kylie nodded again, but inside a tiny voice added, *someone like you, Michael Emerson?*

Something in his face, a slight flicker of disappointment told her that he'd read her thoughts. Warned her that he knew she still harbored a kernel of suspicion somewhere deep inside.

"Why are we stopping?" Nikki shouted, pulling up beside them. Her breathing was more ragged than Kylie's, signaling she was in even worse shape. No big surprise there. They were all city dwellers. None of them were up to Michael's level of physical conditioning. Kylie knew this put more of a burden on him in regards to getting them back safely.

"We're taking a short break to let everyone catch up." He lifted his pole and pointed up the trail. "We should reach the lean-to soon. We'll take a break and figure out where to go from there."

"Any sign of Heather or anyone else having been out here?" Nikki asked.

Michael shook his head and then shouted over the wind, "New snow and the wind have covered everything. If they were out this way, we'll never be able to tell now."

Kylie bit her lip. What about the ski hat? Why was he hiding its existence?

Steven inched his way up to them, his breathing harsh and labored. "Damn, I knew there was a reason my doctor told me to quit my damn smoking." He shoved both poles into the snowpack and leaned forward to rest. "Am I the only one feeling like we're on a wild-goose chase? I vote we head back. I can barely feel my toes."

"Mine went dead twenty minutes ago," Nikki added.

Steven straightened up. "So we're in agreement? We head back?"

Michael shook his head. "We finish what we started. The lean-to is right around the next bend. Heather could have taken shelter there."

Before they could protest, Michael turned and took off, his muscular thighs bunching and knotting, as he skated smoothly, gathering speed.

Kylie felt the tug of the rope around her waist. Time to get moving. She shoved off. She had no other choice than to follow Michael to wherever he was taking them.

THE OUTLINE of the lean-to loomed in the blowing snow. Tucked in neatly between a circle of pines, the familiar structure sent a wave of relief over Michael.

He knew his companions were exhausted. They couldn't go much further without a rest. The lean-to would provide them with a breather, a chance to regroup.

Drifts of snow were piled up against the north end of the building and along the outer lip of the opening. But Michael was certain that once he got a small fire going their moods would lift. The fire wouldn't give them total warmth, but it would be enough to chase off the worst of the chill.

Leaning down, he unsnapped his bindings, picked up his skis and climbed into the interior of the shed. The relentless push and pull of the wind stopped abruptly.

He laid his skis against the side of the building and turned to give Kylie a hand as she scaled the lip of the lean-to. She collapsed against the wall, leaning forward to catch her breath.

Within a few minutes, they were all assembled inside the protection of the lean-to.

"Now what?" Steven demanded.

Michael pointed to the floor. "Someone was here earlier. Snow's been tracked inside. There's footprints."

"But no one is here now," Nikki said.

"No, but whoever was here used the snowshoes." He nodded in the direction of the six pair of snowshoes hanging on hooks against the back wall. Two pair had clumps of snow trapped in their webbing.

Kylie moved over to examine them. She stiffened.

"What's wrong?" he asked.

She reached up and took down one of snowshoes. Her eyes were wide when she turned back. "There's blood on this one."

She held the snowshoe out to him.

Sure enough, several drops of blood stained the aluminum frame. "Damn."

"Now what?"

Michael glanced outside. Gust after gust of wind whipped around the tiny shed, snow swirling and dipping. He could barely make out the partially covered indentation in the snow—a path leading to the gorge.

Someone, most likely whoever had been inside the lean-to, had walked out to the cliffs. Two people.

"I need to check out the gorge." He replaced the blood-stained snowshoe on its hook and took down another pair.

"I'm coming with you," Kylie said, releasing another pair from its place on the wall.

"No, stay with Nikki and get a fire going. Steven can come with me."

"I'm not as winded as he is," Kylie stated, bending down to buckle the snowshoes. "It makes more sense for me to come."

Exasperated at her failure to follow directions, Michael followed suit. Obviously she had her own agenda and listening to him wasn't part of it. He wasn't in the mood to argue.

Nikki moved to the back of the hut, grabbed two more pair off the wall and threw one set to Steven. "Might as well make it a party. We'll come, too."

Michael sighed. So much for anyone taking direction.

A few minutes later, all four of them were headed for the cliff.

As they approached the edge, Michael motioned for them to slow down, to proceed cautiously. Beside him, tension radiated off Kylie.

She didn't speak, but he knew her fear was mounting. Her shoulders were tense, her posture stiff.

He knew she was thinking of the dream. Of her fear of the cliff and its dizzying drop to the gorge below. But he gave her credit, she didn't veer off as they drew closer, she matched him step for step.

He skirted the edge, testing the snow and ice that had accumulated along the rim.

Next to him, Kylie dropped to a squatting position. She shielded her eyes with one hand, peering downward.

Suddenly she rose a little and pointed into the gorge. "Look!"

He leaned out, trying to see through the curtain of snow raining into the gorge.

A sheet of ice, polished and sleek, cascaded in thick layers down the sides of the cliff, reaching all the way to the frozen river below. A deep trough, the sides smooth and glassy, cut through the center of the wash.

Huge cauliflower formations bubbled close to the top of the cliff, and below them, a fragile overhang draped over the trough, a mass of pencil thin icicles beneath. Beautiful but deadly.

Kylie reached up and grabbed his arm. "There, about twenty, thirty feet down!"

He leaned out further and spied what she was pointing at. Something or someone hung deep within the ice trough, the sides curling and cradling the shape.

A blaze of hazy pink shone through the transparent ice.

Heather.

"Damn," he muttered.

"How did she get down there?" Steven yelled over the wind.

Michael shook his head, cupping his hands over his mouth. "I don't know."

"We've got to get her back up here," Kylie shouted. "It doesn't look like she's moving."

Michael nodded, taking quick note of the climbing harness holding Heather in place. It looked as if a single ice screw, driven into the wall a few feet above her, was the only thing holding her suspended in the middle of the channel.

Whoever had left Heather down there was long gone. Either he had climbed back up through the channel or he'd rappelled down to the bottom and walked out.

From the looks of chipped icicles and broken off sections of the cauliflower formations, Michael was betting the person had climbed back up the way he'd gone down.

That made a second descent even more dangerous. The ice looked fragile, damaged.

He shrugged off his backpack and set it at his feet. Unbuckling his snowshoes, he bent down and rummaged through his pack.

"What are you doing?" Kylie asked.

"Going down after her." He pulled out his crampons and quickly fitted them to the bottom of his boots.

Her fingers tightened on his arm, the tips digging frantically into the muscle. "You can't do that. You told me that you're not supposed to be climbing."

He glanced up, allowing their eyes to meet. Snow clung to her hair, strands that had loosened during their trek.

He pulled off his glove and carefully tucked them back under her hat, the tips of his fingers trailing across the silkiness of her skin. She dipped her head for a moment, as if to soak in the touch of his hand.

"We can't leave her down there," he said softly.

Beneath her goggles, her lashes fluttered downward, briefly shielding the resignation, the hopelessness of the situation, hidden in her eyes.

"I know, but—"

"There are no buts, Kylie. I need to do this."

Steven tapped his shoulder. "She's not moving. There's no way she's alive."

A gust of blowing snow slammed into them, cutting off all communication as they huddled down, trying to wait out the bone-rattling attack.

As the force lessened, Michael asked, "Do you want to take the risk that she's alive down there and we walked away?"

The three of them stared mutely at him, each mulling over what he'd asked. He knew from their expressions that they would want someone to come after them if they were the one hanging in the middle of the ice floe.

Finally Kylie cupped her hands over her mouth and shouted, "Tell us what you want us to do."

He grabbed his climbing harness and started buckling it on. He spoke as he suited up, "I'll fix up a relay system. When I get to Heather, I'll tie her off and then release her from the screw holding her in place. You three pull her up. I'll follow behind her."

"What if she's hurt?" Nikki asked, squatting down next to him.

"When she gets up here to the top, Kylie will take over. Get her to the lean-to as quickly as possible. Once I'm up, we'll decide if she can make it back to the lodge on the sled."

Beside him, Kylie dug around in his backpack. "There isn't another rope. Why is there only one climbing rope?"

He didn't look at her but instead concentrated on using the pick to make a good hole for the ice screw. He hammered in the screw and then twisted it until the eye was flush with the surface. He threaded a double length of rope through, anchoring the rope to the top.

"Answer me, Michael."

Instead he knelt close to the edge and studied the ice face, mentally preparing his route down to Heather. He quickly formed a map in his head.

He stood up. "Okay, I'm ready. Let the rope out easy. I'll be using my tools to make my way down. The rope is just in case I slip."

"What happens when you tie Heather off?" Kylie asked, not willing to give up on her previous line of questioning. "What will keep you from falling if she's on the rope?"

He smiled. "Nothing."

"Please tell me you're not serious."

"Don't worry, coming back up will be a piece of cake. I'll easily be able to see where I'm going."

She shook her head, stepping between him and the edge. "No, you can't do this."

He gently moved her aside. "We don't have any other choice, Kylie."

Before she could stop him, he stepped to the edge, moving out onto the ice bubbling over the top.

He skidded across the surface of the cauliflower formations, feeling the friable surface beneath the soles of his feet. He kicked the toe of his left crampon in and fashioned a tentative step.

"Promise me you'll be careful. No heroics."

He glanced into the soulful, penetrating brown of her eyes. There was no missing the fear in her face, the trepidation in her voice.

He nodded. "I promise."

He dropped down over the top, free-falling for a second before hooking his ax around one of the thicker icicles and pulling himself close to the fall.

His rope jumped and skidded over the rough surface overhead until he was able to steady himself.

He pulled the second ax out of his belt, held the shaft parallel to the surface and pick pointed directly into the wall. Ice chips sprayed outward, hitting and stinging his cheeks.

He tapped the front points of his crampons into the ice,

standing upright for balance, his heels low to allow gravity to pull the points deeper into the ice.

Going down an ice fall was harder than going up. There was no way to spot the condition of the ice or to find secure footholds. But Michael knew there was no other way.

The trip down was relatively uneventful, the ice clean and harder than he'd expected. He reached Heather in a matter of minutes and wedged a shoulder into an overhang of ice to rest while reaching out to turn her toward him.

Her body swung lazily in the harness, her head lolled slightly as she turned. When she faced him, Michael realized he didn't need to feel for a pulse. Her eyes were wide-open and staring, crystals forming on her eyelashes and around her mouth. Her skin held a bluish white cast.

She was dead.

"Is she okay?" Kylie shouted from above.

He looked up.

Kylie was lying on her stomach, her head and shoulders appearing over the edge. Her expression was eager, her anticipation high that they had arrived in time.

Michael shook his head, watching the eagerness on her face fade. She pulled back and he knew she was hiding her disappointment. Her fear. It was possible that they were all facing another murder.

He quickly tied the rope to Heather's harness and released her from the ice screw. The rope drew taut, telling the three above that they now controlled Heather's ascent out of the gorge.

He cupped his hands. "Pull her up!"

Kylie's head appeared over the rim again and she nodded. The determination on her face told him she'd recovered. She was back in rescue mode. She signaled to Steven and Nikki to begin reeling Heather up.

Michael watched as the body started up, the ascent smooth and effortless. Until he noticed the thick icicle projecting from a ledge ten feet above him. Heather's body was headed directly for it. The possibility of her snagging on the icicle worried him.

He tipped his head back and tried to yell, but Heather's body hit the icicle hard. An audible crack split the air and a huge chunk broke off.

The projectile fell, spiraling downward.

"Look out!" Kylie yelled.

Michael tried to swing to the left but he wasn't quick enough.

The heavy dagger slammed into his right shoulder, throwing him off balance. A burst of pain radiated down his arm and into his fingers, making them numb and forcing him to lose his grip on the ax.

His right foot slipped and he grabbed for the ax as it fell. But the numbness in his arm made him clumsy. The pick end of the ax stabbed the heel of his hand through his glove as it spun past, hitting the wall and tumbling out into space.

He hung from the left ax, his feet scrambling frantically for footing. The falling pick bounced along the wall, sending a shower of ice shards arching outward, until finally it shot into the gorge below.

His right arm hung at his side, the only sensation a slight tingling in the wrist. Michael was fairly certain feeling would return, but until it did, he had only his feet and left arm to complete the climb.

His left arm was already screaming with fatigue.

He tipped his head back and looked up. The others had hauled Heather's body over the lip.

He wedged his shoulder behind one of the bigger icicles on the left and rested. Air raced in and out of his lungs. Blood pounded in his ears.

Leaning forward, he rested his forehead against the wall, the cold of the ice seeping through the knit of his cap to soothe the beads of sweat that trickled down the side of his face.

He'd been in worse situations, life-threatening, on-the-edge climbing conditions. This was minor in comparison. If he could just rest for a moment, he knew he could muster the strength to complete the climb.

But even as he whispered assurances, a heavy veil of fatigue pressed in on him. Hard. Draining.

A familiar pain, sharp and unrelenting, jumped into existence, centering between his eyes. His vision blurred and the ice fall faded to a hazy mass of polished white.

He sucked in cold air. Maybe he had miscalculated. Maybe he wouldn't make it this time.

KYLIE TORE OFF her ski glove and pressed her fingers to Heather's neck. Nothing. The woman's cold skin and paper-white complexion told her what she already knew. She was gone.

Steven squatted down next to her. "Something's wrong. Michael isn't moving."

Kylie crawled to the edge of the cliff, hanging onto the rope as she peeked over. Michael was pressed close to the fall, his head resting against it. He wasn't moving.

She motioned toward Heather. "Untie the rope from Heather."

Nikki and Steven scrambled to obey. They threw it to her.

Kylie flipped the rope overhand into the gorge. The colorful nylon sailed outward, uncoiling as it fell to dangle a few inches from Michael. He turned his head, but made no move to grab it.

"Grab it, Michael!" Nikki yelled.

He shifted his weight but for some reason seemed unable to reach for the rope.

"He isn't moving his right arm." Kylie pulled back, staring at her two companions as concern raced up the center of her spine. "The icicle must have hit him harder than we thought. He's injured."

"What are we going to do?" Steven yelled over the howl of the wind.

Kylie yanked the rope back up.

"What the hell are you doing?" Nikki screamed, clawing at her arm. "You're going to kill him!"

"Let go," Kylie shouted. "He's hurt. He can't tie himself off with one arm. One of us is going to have to climb down."

The other two looked at her as if she'd grown another head. Neither spoke.

Kylie grabbed a harness and a carabiner. She threaded the rope through and secured herself.

Kneeling down, she rummaged through Michael's backpack. There had to be another pair of crampons. He wouldn't have come out here without them.

A spike stabbed her finger. Good man, she thought as she pulled the extra pair out of the bag. She crouched down and strapped them onto her boots, her fingers clumsy and awkward from the cold.

She pulled her gloves on, tucking her hands under her arms in attempt to warm them.

"You can't be thinking about going down there," Steven yelled in her ear.

She glanced up at him. "Not if you're prepared to volunteer."

He stepped back, his hands going up in protest. "I'm not that insane."

She wasn't surprised. As much as she had hoped he'd agree to go, she knew from his expression that he was as frightened as she was at the prospect of descending into the gorge. So much for chivalry.

"Well, I guess that leaves me then," she said.

Standing up, she grabbed the two other ice axes lying on the ground and shoved them into the belt around her waist.

She moved to the edge of the cliff, trying without success not to look down. Snow and ice spit from beneath her crampons, spinning out into space.

She squeezed her eyes shut as a wave of dizziness slammed into her. Shots of nausea-producing adrenaline squirted into her tender belly.

Please, she prayed, *let me do this without puking all over myself.*

Nikki tapped her shoulder. "Do you know what you're doing?"

"Not by a long shot, but I've got to give it a try."

She swallowed, ignoring the dryness that made her throat ache. "No way am I leaving him down there."

Nikki nodded, a touch of something close to respect entering her green eyes. "Tell me what you want us to do."

"You're going to need to lower me down. I know a few

things about ice climbing, but I'm not an expert by a long shot." Kylie moved to the crest. "Hopefully I know enough to get me through this."

She paused on the edge, her toes cramping and aching in the toe box of her boot. Her pulse slammed against the sides of her head.

Without looking, she sucked in a fortifying breath and dropped over the side.

Her heart jumped into her throat and sweat coated her palm. She started going sideways, her body slipping, but she tightened her grip on the rope and quickly righted herself.

"Easy does it," she whispered. "You can do this."

From below, Michael shouted up, "Don't come down!"

She ignored him, moving cautiously down the ice fall, her feet finding footholds with surprising ease.

A few minutes later, she was beside him. "Fancy meeting you here."

"What the hell are you doing?" he demanded, his words stiff and angry. He wasn't happy.

His face was gray with sweat, his eyelashes and the fringe of hair sticking from beneath his hat wet. Fatigue lined his lean face, and there was no missing the pain in his eyes.

"Nice way to greet a gal," she said breezily. She wedged her crampons in tight and dropped her heels, getting a good stance. "You ready to get out of here?"

"You should have waited. I'd have gotten up."

"Heck, Michael, it was time for me to conquer that silly fear of mine. I thought I'd come down and join you. How's the arm?"

"The feeling still isn't back. I thought if I gave it a few minutes it would come back enough for me to use it."

"No problem," she said, moving closer. "We'll go up together."

She grabbed the carabiner dangling from his waist and clipped it to hers, securing them both to the rope.

"Use your good arm," she instructed, pulling out her own ice axes and sinking them into the ice face level with his left one.

Together they started up the trough of ice, their feet moving in unison, timing their strikes into the ice face with their picks perfectly.

As they neared the top, the rope tightened as Steven and Nikki pulled them to safety. They collapsed on the snow, their breathing labored.

He turned his head toward her. "Thanks."

She grinned. "I don't think I'll let you forget it. Something tells me it will make for an interesting article in *ADVENTURE* magazine—Novice Climber Saves Adrenaline Junkie Michael Emerson's Sorry Butt."

"I'll never work in this town again."

"Good. You're not supposed to be climbing in case you've forgotten."

Stumbling slightly, they stood up. Steven and Nikki moved to give them a hand.

Kylie stopped. The sight of Heather's body lying a few feet away halted her lighthearted exchange, reminding her why they had made the climb in the first place.

She glanced at Michael, noting the expression of dreaded anticipation on his face. No doubt he was thinking the same thing she was. They were returning to the hotel with another dead woman in their possession.

Kylie hadn't liked the way Denner had handled things

up to this point. But the fact remained, they were returning with Michael's ski cap, a cap found lying on the very same trail Heather had taken earlier in the day.

It pretty much guaranteed that the New York City detective had the absolute right and obligation to question Michael about his possible involvement in Heather's death.

Kylie could only hope that Michael had a good explanation for the detective and the rest of them.

Chapter Nine

As Michael expected, Denner went after him with a vengeance once they arrived back at the lodge, but not before Heather's body was placed in one of the adjacent sheds. According to Denner, the cold would preserve any evidence until the local crime scene investigators could make it back out to the lodge.

Once this was accomplished, the police detective spent a good two hours questioning all of them individually.

For some reason, Michael didn't tell him about his ski cap. Somehow he couldn't—no, wouldn't—give the cop more ammunition. Not until he figured out who in the group was setting him up to take the fall.

He watched Kylie when she came out of the library, trying to read her expression and figure out how much she'd revealed. But she kept her face carefully averted from his.

Although, since Denner didn't seem any closer to nailing him, Michael figured she'd kept his counsel. He wasn't sure why. He knew she was still suspicious of him. Her hot and cold reaction to him made that pretty clear.

Following the questioning, they had all congregated in the lobby, waiting for Sara to announce dinner. Nikki had the rest of us do. Besides, dinner should be ready in a few minutes and everyone can concentrate on that rather than needling each other."

"Thanks, but I think I'm going to skip dinner. I'm going to head out to the cabin."

"No way." He shook off Nikki's hand and stood up. "The storm's gotten too bad and there's no heat out there."

"I'll be fine. I'll get a good fire going and keep warm that way."

"Absolutely not." He clenched his back teeth in preparation for battle. No way was he backing down on this issue. She might have ignored his directions out at the cliffs, but he wasn't going to let it happen now. There was no way he was letting her out of his sight. "You need to stay here in the lodge."

"My stuff is out in the cabin," she protested.

"So we'll pack it up and bring it in here."

"I have to agree with Emerson," Denner said. He'd been quiet up to this point, taking in their bickering and complaining with a certain amount of amusement. "Until I know what the hell is going on around here, we're all going to stick together. No one leaves the lodge."

"The only room left is the Whiteface Suite," Templer announced. "All the other rooms are closed off. Unless you want to sleep in Heather's old room."

"Thanks, but I'll pass." Her pained expression told Michael that she was working to suppress a shudder.

"Fine. You can take the Whiteface Suite," he said.

"You do realize, of course, that the Whiteface suite is our most expensive suite of rooms?" The haughty quality of Templer's voice grated on Michael's nerves.

"And how exactly is that a problem?" he asked. "Because I *know* you wouldn't be stupid enough to think you're going to charge her for the suite."

Templer raised an eyebrow, indicating he intended to do just that. "This is a hotel, Mr. Emerson, not a homeless shelter."

"Fine, put it on my bill," Michael snapped. He was ticked he was getting as irritated and annoyed as the rest of them. Cabin fever gone amok.

"There's no need to do that. I'm perfectly capable of paying my own way," Kylie said.

Great. He'd managed to offend her. "Of course you can. No one doubts that. But since it's the hotel's fault that there's no heat in your father's cabin, I'll make arrangements for the board of directors to comp you a room for the rest of your stay. It's the least we can do."

"The storm is responsible for the loss of electricity, not the hotel," Templer said stiffly. He ignored Michael's pointed stare and turned to Nikki. "Perhaps you and your sister would prefer to stay in the Whiteface suite, Ms. Greenley. Ms. McKee could take one of your rooms."

"Forget it!" Gracie said, jumping to her feet. "There is no way I'm staying in that suite."

Michael shot a quick glance in Gracie's direction. What the hell was wrong with her? She acted as if the man had told her that she'd have to sleep in the equipment shed. Was everyone going off the deep end at once?

"Relax, Gracie, no one is forcing you to move," he reassured her. "Kylie can stay in the Whiteface suite. I'll even help her move her things in. You stay where you are."

Gracie, however, seemed oblivious to what he said. Her

face was a mask of panic. She paced up and down the floor, her jaw tightening as she gnawed on the side of her cheek. Michael figured that if she kept it up she was going to wear a hole right through to the outside.

Next to him, Nikki sighed, her exasperation with her sister obvious. She nudged him and glanced skyward, her meaning apparent. *Just ignore her. It's Gracie being Gracie.*

He shook his head, warning her to lay off. She stuck her lip out in a typical Nikki pout, but seemed willing to keep quiet for the moment.

He got up and went to Gracie, reaching out to stop her restless pacing. "Come on, kiddo, what's wrong? You're wound so tight you're ready to burst. "

"It's—it's just that I hate those rooms. I can't stay in them."

"And I already said you don't have to. Relax. It's all going to work out fine."

"You should gut the whole suite and start over," she said, the viciousness in her voice surprising him.

"A little over the top maybe, but I get the message—no Whiteface Suite for you."

"Don't bother trying to understand her, Michael," Nikki chimed in, her moratorium on Gracie insults obviously over. "My darling, slightly demented sister has a phobia about that suite. She hasn't set foot in them for eleven years."

Michael glanced at her, an eyebrow raised. As expected, Nikki was only too willing to continue. "Those are the rooms we stayed in when we were kids—kind of our family's unofficial summer residence. At least they were until our parents built their own house."

She sat back and with exaggerated slowness crossed her long legs, allowing one foot to swing jauntily. Sensuously. Michael knew it was for his benefit. She enjoyed being in the spotlight.

"In fact, Gracie only slept there once after the accident." She threw her head back and shook out her hair, taking her time for full effect. "Shortly after midnight, she woke up screaming and claimed that Andrea was in the room."

Michael quickly glanced at Kylie. Her face had gone white, her eyes round. He watched as she absently lifted a hand and chewed a nail.

Great, now she was spooked. If things kept up she wouldn't have a single nail left by the end of the week.

"Naturally, Mom freaked and Daddy lost it." Nikki's smile widened, all white teeth with the slightest hint of perverse pleasure curling her bottom lip. "Daddy made sure Gracie never had to sleep in that suite again. He—uh, how should I put this delicately—sent Gracie away the very next day. Claimed she needed a—" She used her fingers to make quotations in the air. *"Rest."*

She laughed again and the sound hung in the room unchallenged. Several of the guests and staff looked away, as if sensing Gracie's embarrassment.

"What was the name of that place Daddy sent you to, Gracie? Brattle Rest Home? Bratten Retreat?"

"Brattenhurst Retreat," Gracie answered softly. She didn't look up, but instead, stood with her head down, her hands clasped tightly across her upper chest. She looked beaten, humiliated.

Nikki snapped her fingers. "That's right, Brattenhurst

Retreat! Pleasant little place tucked away in a quiet, unassuming corner of Vermont. Lots of green grass, cute little park benches under oak trees and quaint brick buildings." She sat forward, a malicious glint in her eyes. She was in major attack mode.

"Of course," Nikki added, "the place was a bit of a downer, what with its locked wards and more shrinks per square foot than the Hamptons during the entire month of August."

She sat back again, her grin self-satisfied. Bitchy. "But then our little Gracie enjoyed that part of it, didn't you, Gracie? All that attention. All those people pampering you. How many times have you been back for a *visit?* Ten? Twenty? Thirty times?"

"T-they've helped me a lot," Gracie stammered. She lifted her head and stared straight ahead.

Gracie's comment seemed to snap Kylie out of her freeze. She glared at Nikki. "I think that's about enough," she said. She walked over to stand next to her friend, her arm going up to gently touch her shoulder. Gracie jumped, but her gaze softened.

Kylie leaned in. "Ignore her. She's just being cruel. You've gone through a lot over the years. I'm glad you've gotten the help you need."

Gracie nodded mutely, her throat convulsing. No sound came out.

"Oh, will you stop babying her? She loves that. I'm tired of everyone tiptoeing around my crazy sister. She goes around the bend about every six months or so."

She stood up, walked over to the bar and grabbed a glass. With quick, efficient movements, she poured herself a generous splash of white wine. She held up the goblet. "Anyone care to join me?"

No one responded and Gracie's shoulders shook beneath Kylie's hand. She was sobbing without making a sound.

Nikki snorted in disgust and took a defiant sip. "Great, now she's crying. Stop sniffling, Gracie. Don't you know it's fashionable to have a nervous breakdown? Everyone is having one these days."

"Drop it, Nikki," Michael ordered.

"Oh great, now you've got Michael joining in on the *Gracie pity party.* It's always about you, isn't it, Gracie? Just because this was supposed to be my weekend, you had to butt in and ruin it."

Nikki took another swallow of wine and returned to her perch on the couch. She stared sulkily at the fire, her tirade apparently finished. Mission accomplished. She'd reduced her sister to tears and shocked the rest of the group into stunned silence.

"Come on, Gracie, let's get our coats," Kylie said, guiding her friend toward the hall leading to the kitchen. "You can come out to the cabin and help me pack a few things."

Michael moved to follow. "I'll help."

Kylie shot him a warning glance that stopped him dead in his tracks. "Thanks, but I think we can handle this on our own. We'll meet you all for dinner later."

They left the room, leaving him to deal with Nikki.

A FEW HOURS LATER, her bag packed and sitting a few feet away, Kylie sat alone on the bottom step of the main staircase.

She had hoped to have a heart-to-heart talk with Gracie, but her old friend had given her the slip shortly after exiting the lobby. She had complained of feeling tired and escaped upstairs, curtailing any opportunity to chat.

So, Kylie had been left to pack her belongings alone and return to the hotel for the night. Leaving the tiny cabin behind hadn't been easy. She would have preferred to stay there in spite of the cold. Anything to avoid the insipid bickering Nikki and her cronies seemed to enjoy so much. If this was how the wealthy spent their vacations, she was glad she didn't have two nickels to rub together.

From down the hall, she could hear the muffled voices of the others filtering from beneath the kitchen door. They were eating a late dinner, taking the opportunity to go over the day's events.

Everyone had a theory about what was going on, but in reality none of them had a clue. Their fear of who was going to get picked off next was beginning to wear the veneer of civility thin.

But perhaps even more frightening was the way they looked at each other, wondering which of them was the killer.

Although Kylie had tried to follow the discussion over dinner, she had quickly reached a point and had to escape. The knowledge that Michael's ski hat remained jammed deep inside the pocket of his ski jacket hung on her like a weight.

She'd been unable to meet his eyes across the table in spite of the fact that he'd tried more than once to connect with her several times during the meal.

Finally, unable to handle the tension, she had excused herself and escaped. She needed time to think. Needed time to decide what she would do next.

In the corner of the lobby, the elegant wood-grain clock ticked off the minutes. The gold pendulum in the base of the clock swished back and forth soundlessly. From her perch on the bottom step, Kylie watched its hypnotic dance.

Seconds passed and the silence of the empty lobby pressed in on her.

She jumped when the clock broke the silence. Ten evenly spaced bongs. Ten o'clock.

It was late. The day had come and gone in a flash and another person lay dead. None of them had been able to sleep last night, a sense of desperate panic seeming to infuse the air of the old lodge.

Exhausted, she leaned forward and rested her forehead on her knees. The cloth of her ski pants, smooth and sleek, cooled her hot cheeks.

Then she sat up and rested the small of her back against the hardwood stair. She was so tired she could barely think, let alone make a coherent decision. Every muscle in her body ached from strenuous skiing and the climb.

But no amount of fatigue changed the fact that Heather was gone. That her body lay wrapped in a tarp in the outer shed. She was dead. Murdered.

And Kylie knew that the *only* person at the hotel who had the expertise and skill to suspend Heather's body in the middle of the ice fall was Michael Emerson. Her heart thudded against her breastbone, the rhythm in sync with the tick of the clock.

What was she supposed to do? She couldn't simply deny the inevitable. She had to tell Denner what she knew.

Behind her, the whirl of gears signaled the sound of the elevator starting up. She lifted her head. Who was foolish enough to use the elevator? Everyone knew it wasn't functioning right.

The floor numbers above the doors lit up. The elevator was descending.

Four…

No one was supposed to be on the fourth floor.

Three…

Who was in it?

Two…

Almost here.

One…

The bell dinged and the doors slid open. Frigid air, sharp and bitter, rushed out and brushed her cheek with an eerie chill.

She leaned forward, straining to see inside.

The chamber was empty. The lights inside muted, glowing a soft yellowish tint. Something primal stirred deep inside her, and the hair on the back of her neck rose.

"Kyyyyyylie—"

The childish voice rode the crest of the chilly air. The wispy tendrils of hair tucked behind her ear stirred and rustled softly.

She tightened her fingers over her knees, trying to anchor herself to the step. Her heart beat faster and she squeezed her eyes shut. You don't hear anything, she whispered to herself. No one is calling your name.

"Kyyyyyylie—"

She stood up; her hand fumbled for the railing. Her fingers, tingling with anticipation, slid along the smooth, polished wood.

"Kyyyyyylie—"

As if in a trance, her feet moved, one foot in front of the other. All other sounds vanished, swallowed into a swirling vapor of nothingness.

Suddenly she was inside the elevator. The walls pressed in on her and time stretched, slowing to a crawl.

As if from a great distance away, she watched a hand—her own hand—reach up and press the button for the fourth floor.

The doors rolled shut and the elevator lurched upward. She stumbled backward, pressing her spine to the elevator wall. Beneath the paneling, the gears shifted and the wall vibrated and throbbed. The lights overhead seemed overly bright and painfully sharp.

Her mouth went dry, as if she'd eaten sand. All moisture gone in a single instant. Even if she could have pried her lips open, she knew no words would come. She was mute. And totally alone.

The floor of the elevator shuttered beneath her feet, and the doors slid open. She was on the fourth floor.

Light from the elevator spilled out into the dark, empty hall. The only sound was the muted whine of the generator pumping heat through the ducts in the walls of the old hotel.

Her breath, raspy and rough, spilled from between her lips in a thin white vapor. No heat was reaching the fourth floor. Her fingertips tingled from the cold dampness.

She stepped out into the hall. Water squished beneath her feet, seeping out beneath the edges of the rug onto the hardwood floor. Like before, it froze, turning a pale crystalized white as soon as it hit the air.

Her heart slammed against her upper chest and blood pounded in her ears. She glanced down the corridor.

Yellow light spilled into the hall from the open door of room 416. Someone had left the light on.

The length of the hall seemed to shift. Narrowing. Stretching out in front of her. Her feet shuffled as if under their own power, moving her down the corridor until she stood before the open door.

The crime scene tape was ripped, the strips hanging limp against the door frame.

Slowly, cautiously, she eased into the room.

"Hello?" Her voice shook, sounding small and timid. "Is anyone in here?"

Silence.

The room was empty.

She turned to leave but stopped when something cold brushed across the back of her neck. A rash of goose bumps pebbled across her neck and arms.

A soft bluish glow filled the room and the figure of a small child appeared, the outline of her body faint, indistinct, airy.

"Andrea?" The name slipped out, whispered on the back of Kylie's tortured breath.

The figure smiled, a wistful upward curl of her transparent lips. The smile was sweet, filled with the promise of eternal childhood.

"What is it?" Kylie stepped closer, ignoring the tremors that shook her body. "What do you want from me?"

The drapes over the window rustled and moved as if riding on the wind of a soft breeze. The hem drifted lazily across the floor.

Her heart pounded as a thin vaporous mist coated the window pane, as if someone had breathed upon the cold glass with their warm breath.

She watched in horror as something—someone—spelled out the words:

HELP ME, KYLIE
FIND THE NOTE

Oh, God, this couldn't be happening. There was no such thing as ghosts.

Air shuddered in and out of her lungs.

Andrea's figure shimmered and the bluish glow intensified. A sheen of ice formed on the window, obliterating the words.

Slowly Andrea faded and the room went dark.

Her heart accelerated to a mad gallop. She turned and stumbled into the hall.

To the left, the elevator door stood open.

No way was she getting in that thing again.

She swung to the right, her gaze locating the comforting glow of the exit sign at the opposite end of the hall. She took off, her feet hitting the carpet with a thunderous beat.

Breathless, she reached the door, the palm of her hand hitting the release bar with a satisfying smack. The door swung open and she tumbled through, slamming into something solid. Unmovable.

Arms surrounded her, enclosing her with a strength that was frightening. She wiggled to get away, but she was trapped. Held captive.

"Let me go!" Her struggles turned frantic.

But the arms tightened around her, holding her firmly. She tried to drop down beneath the arms, but the hold only seemed to tighten.

"Relax, Kylie. It's me." His hand came up to hold her head to his chest.

She collapsed against him, feeling the reassuring beat of his heart against her ear.

Michael. Oh God, it was Michael. Relief washed over her and she leaned back to drink him in, savoring the deep concern in his eyes as he gently stroked her hair and tried to impart some of his own calm composure into her wildly beating heart.

As she leaned against him, she could feel a sense of calm wash over her and that surprised her. How had this man managed to get under her skin so quickly that just his presence gave her peace?

"What the hell happened?"

"I—I don't know." She shook her head, confusion clouding her brain. "One minute I was sitting in the lobby and the next thing I knew, I was coming up here."

He touched the side of her face, the sensation of his fingers warm and gentle against her cool skin. For a moment, she thought her heart might melt into a puddle of emotion right there on the fourth floor of the hotel. But she quickly shored up her defenses and began questioning her sanity.

What was happening to her? Where had her earlier suspicions gone? How was it possible that she vacillated so quickly between thinking he could be the killer and finding safety in his arms? Was this place truly getting to her?

"Come on, something must have happened. You were scared out of your wits."

She opened her mouth to tell him, to describe to him how Andrea had again appeared, this time requesting her help to find some kind of note. A note that might possibly explain the murders.

But something stopped her, froze the words to the tip of her tongue. How could she tell him that she'd seen Andrea again? He'd think she was a nut case for sure.

Besides, he'd already told her last night that he didn't believe in ghosts. Never mind the fact that *she* didn't believe in ghosts.

She gnawed her bottom lip. *Think, woman, think.* There had to be another explanation. She was overtired. Distraught. What she needed was a good night's sleep. She'd see things more clearly in the morning. After that maybe she'd be able to talk to him about the fourth floor. But not now. Definitely not now.

"You know what? I am way too overtired." She rubbed a spot between her eyes. "Too much excitement for one day."

"You're copping out on me. Tell me what scared you so badly."

She ducked her head. "I thought I heard something and came up to investigate." She gave a shaky laugh. "Pretty stupid, huh?"

He frowned. "What are you not telling me?"

"Nothing. It's just as I said—I got spooked."

She stepped back out of his embrace and immediately regretted the loss of warmth, the rejection of the protection he offered.

She paused, her gaze drawn to the window in the heavy door overlooking the darkened corridor beyond. Even through the heavy glass, she could see the shadows in the hall. As she watched, they seemed to lengthen and slide along the edges of the floor.

She wet her lips, her mouth suddenly dry.

If she didn't know better, she could have sworn that the shadows were curling and snaking down the sides of the hall, hugging the edges of the rug as they moved in their direction.

A chilliness, something cold and infinitely dank and disturbing, grabbed at her ankles and slipped up the length of her legs.

She shuddered and turned away. "Let's get out of here. This place is creeping me out."

Before he could respond, she started down the stairs, taking them two at a time. Whatever was lurking in that corridor wasn't going to pull her back. Not this time anyway.

AS SHE ROUNDED the landing leading to the lobby, Kylie wasn't surprised to find Denner standing at the bottom. He lounged against the carved pillar, his arms folded across his barrel chest and his expression amused. Expectant.

"Having a little rendezvous with your number one fan, Emerson? Making sure she's got her story straight?"

"What story would that be?" Michael asked casually, his tone implying his weariness of Denner's constant badgering.

"Where you were all morning before Ms. Barlowe disappeared?"

"I was in the library with Kylie most of the morning. But then you know that as well as I do."

"Yeah, makes things real convenient for you, doesn't it?"

Michael's hands tightened into fists and he brushed past her to stand in front of the detective. He was on the step above him so he towered over the older man. But even if they'd been standing toe-to-toe, Kylie was sure from the expression on Michael's face that he'd win any contest of intimidation.

"Tell me this, Denner, have you even bothered to talk to anyone besides me?"

The detective laughed. "Why? What would be the point? You and I both know who's responsible."

Irritated and still shaky from her encounter upstairs, Kylie hurried down the final few steps. "If you two don't mind, I'm not going to stick around for this conversation. Personally I've had about all I can take of your bickering. Another woman's dead and we have no leads."

She hit Denner with a look of disdain. "I'd have thought that having a policeman around would have assured the rest of us of making it through this storm alive. Guess I was wrong."

Knowing she didn't want to run into the crowd still congregated in the kitchen, Kylie headed across the lobby. Maybe the library was empty. She needed some time away from everyone, time to figure out what Andrea had been trying to tell her.

"Kylie, wait," Michael called after her. "We need—"

She waved him off. "Not now. I need some time alone."

She swung through the archway and headed down the hall to the library. As she passed the door to the Fitness/Spa, she stopped, surprised to find it partially open.

The sound of weights clanking against each other slipped through the open crack. Someone was working out.

Curious, she pushed open the door.

Gracie sat with her back to the door, hunched over a weight machine's padded platform, her hands grasping two handles. The thin straps of her workout top did nothing to conceal the heavy sheen of perspiration coating her upper body.

She grunted slightly as she lifted the weights, the well-developed muscles of her neck, shoulders and upper arms standing out in stark relief. Gracie wasn't the washed-out lump she appeared to be.

Kylie stepped inside. "I didn't know you were a gym rat."

The weights hit the rack with a resounding clank. Gracie turned. "I—I didn't hear you come in."

"You were too absorbed in your workout." She walked over to stand on the opposite side of the bicep machine. "When did you start training?"

Gracie grabbed a Nike warm-up jacket and quickly slipped it on. "Oh, I don't really train. Just fool around once in a while when I'm bored." She pulled the towel off the top of the machine and used the end to blot the beads of sweat streaming down the sides of her neck.

Kylie grinned and pointed to her upper arm. "Your muscles say otherwise."

She gentled the intensity of her grin, suddenly aware that Gracie wasn't comfortable with her praise. She sought to put her at ease by folding her arms on top of the machine and casually resting her chin on one fist.

"Don't be embarrassed. I'm envious. I'm always promising myself that this is the year I'm going to get into shape." She shrugged. "But it never seems to happen."

"That's because you're attending medical school. Making something out of your life instead of wasting it like a lot of us."

"What I'm doing is making the student loan program rich. At the rate I'm going I'll be paying off loans until I'm eighty."

"Still worth it when you consider what you're doing with your life."

Gracie threw the towel over one shoulder and walked over to the window. She snatched a water bottle off the ledge and used her teeth to pry open the top. Tilting her head back, she took a long gulp.

Her green eyes lifted to meet Kylie's. "You know what?"

"What?"

"I used to promise myself that I'd go to college. That I'd do something important with my life." Her shoulders slumped and her posture took on its familiar defeated look. To Kylie, the change was in stark contrast to the confident pumped-up person who had sat in front of the exercise machine a few moments ago.

Gracie shrugged. "But it's never going to happen."

"Of course it'll happen. It has already. Nikki said earlier that you were involved in charitable work. That's important. It's the kind of thing that makes a difference."

"Yeah, right. What I do is busywork for rich girls who have too much time on their hands. Makes us feel as though we're contributing. But we aren't fooling anyone. Least of all ourselves."

"What makes you say that? If people aren't willing to work to raise money for charitable organizations there wouldn't be anything going on in the field of medical research." Kylie paused for a moment and then added, "Or in the area of health care for the poor."

From her expression, it was obvious that Gracie wasn't buying anything she said. A sense of despondency seemed to fill the room.

Kylie leaned forward. "The government isn't going to

make all that stuff happen, Gracie. There just isn't enough money to go around. But you and other people make it possible."

Gracie laughed, the sound dismissive. "It's obvious that you've bought the usual line of charitable bull. We do what we do so that we have another excuse to dress up in expensive designer gowns, drape ourselves in useless jewelry and stare at platters of exorbitantly priced food. Food that ends up in the trash at the end of the event because none of the women dare to eat anything for fear of losing their perfect anorexic figures."

The bitterness in Gracie's words struck a cord deep within Kylie. She walked over to stand a few inches from her friend. "I don't think I've ever heard anyone describe charitable works in quite that way before."

"Maybe because all us charity gals work so hard to keep the true reason for our *work* a dark, dirty secret."

Gracie glanced away as if unable to meet her gaze, her mouth twisted into a grimace of such self-hatred that Kylie wasn't sure how to respond.

"What's happened to you, Gracie?"

"Nothing. This is me. This is who I am."

Kylie squatted down in front of her friend and slipped her hand through hers, wrapping her fingers over the large, rough hand. Through force of will, she tried to reestablish eye contact. But Gracie kept her face averted.

She tried to reach out with words, "When we were kids, you never let anything get you down. You were always so full of feisty determination. What changed?"

She wondered if Gracie's totally defeated attitude was recent. The result of her father's untimely death perhaps.

Could she be clinically depressed? Certainly Nikki's cruel revelations concerning Gracie's emotional struggles and her frequent admissions for treatment indicated she was vulnerable to such a diagnosis.

Gracie didn't respond.

"I heard of your father's death, but I don't know what happened. Do you want to talk about it?"

Her friend's head turned a fraction of an inch, her gaze flicking in Kylie's direction for a brief second and then away again. She opened her mouth as if to speak but no words came out.

"It's okay to talk about it. Tell me what happened."

"Why don't you ask Michael?" Gracie's voice was sharp with undisguised resentment.

"Why should I ask Michael?"

Gracie turned to stare directly into her face. Kylie was surprised to see that her eyes were filled with such rage, such hatred that she was hard-pressed not to pull back.

"Because he's the one responsible for my father's death."

Kylie paused, totally confused. What was Gracie talking about? She wasn't making any sense.

"I don't understand. How is Michael responsible?"

Gracie latched on to Kylie's forearm, her fingers digging into the skin so hard Kylie had to bite her lip to keep from crying out.

"Because if he hadn't agreed to take my father on his last climb, my father would still be alive."

Understanding dawned, and Kylie sank down onto the floor. Of course, why hadn't she put the pieces together earlier? Arthur Greenley, Gracie and Nikki's father, had been the *old friend* who had died on Michael's last climb.

The memory of the newspaper article jumped into Kylie's consciousness. The reporter had written about a terrible accident involving an unskilled climber who had taken an ill-fated chance and fallen over a hundred feet. The article described how Michael Emerson had made a heroic attempt to save the climber, but in the end, failed, his actions resulting in his own accident.

"I'm sorry. I had no idea it was your father who died during Michael's climb six months ago. I knew someone had been killed and Michael had gotten injured but..."

The strength of Gracie's grip lessened and she stood up. There was no lessening of the rage that seemed to consume her, though. She stepped over Kylie and started to pace the floor, her movements tight and jerky, barely controlled.

"I told him not to go. Begged him actually." She ran a restless hand through her hair, her expression tortured. "But it was like he was having some kind of midlife crisis. He wouldn't listen to reason. It was as if he had to prove something to himself."

"This must have been hell on your family, Gracie."

She whirled around. "Hell? You don't know what hell is! I wanted to—" Her face froze and she clamped her lips shut, cutting off her own words.

"You wanted to what?" Kylie asked softly, wanting her friend to continue to talk, to get out the venom that seemed to be eating her alive.

"Nothing." Gracie waved a hand, dismissing her. "You wouldn't understand."

"Give me a chance. Tell me so I can try to understand."

"You want to understand? Really understand?"

Kylie nodded.

Gracie snatched hp her water bottle and towel. "If Michael Emerson hadn't planned that stupid party eleven years ago my little sister would be alive today. And if he hadn't taken my father with him on his last climb then my father would still be alive too. He managed to wipe out half of my family. How's that for true Emerson selfishness?"

"You and I weren't *forced* to go to that party, Gracie. We made a bad decision and we bear some responsibility."

"You think I don't know that?" Gracie's voice was bitterly cutting.

"Everyone who attended that party knew what they were doing."

"Everyone except Andrea."

Kylie nodded. "Yes, Andrea was a true innocent. But if Nikki hadn't left her with us and taken off, and if you and I had done what we were supposed to do, then maybe none of us would be feeling so guilty right now. But we were kids and kids make mistakes."

"Well, if Michael hadn't sent a note demanding Nikki meet up with him, she wouldn't have relied on me to watch Andrea."

"But none of it was done on purpose, Gracie. We were all selfish and self-centered back then. We were kids. If we knew what we do now, none of us would have planned to go to the party. But we made a mistake—Michael for planning the party and you and me for not paying attention to Andrea. We all paid the price. Maybe it's time to let things go."

"You're right. It is time to let things go. Mainly because no one gets it and none of it matters anymore."

Kylie stood up, moving toward her friend. "But it does matter. It matters to me."

She touched Gracie's shoulder, trying desperately to keep her from shutting her out. "We don't have to talk about Andrea or your dad if you don't want to. Just stay for a bit."

But Gracie didn't respond, her facial features closed.

Kylie tried again. "I've wanted to apologize for a long time for not staying in contact with you after the accident. I should have been a better friend."

Gracie turned toward her again, her gaze softer, and for a moment, Kylie thought she might actually talk. That she might open up.

Tears swam along the lower rim of her eyes and her lower lip trembled slightly. But then, just as quickly as the tears appeared, she blinked and they vanished.

"It's a two-way street, Kylie. I could have picked up the phone just as easily as you. Guess we both got busy with our lives and forgot." She shrugged. "No harm done."

"From the sounds of things, a lot of harm was done."

Gracie laughed, the sound absent of humor. "Don't be so melodramatic. Life goes on."

With that final dismissal, she turned and left, leaving Kylie to contemplate what had happened between them. The pain and anger that lurked so quietly beneath the surface of her former childhood friend shocked her.

What did it all mean and how was it related to what was happening at Cloudspin?

Chapter Ten

Kylie swung her duffel bag up onto the bed and stepped back to survey her new living quarters. Impressive. Actually more than impressive. It was all a bit overwhelming. The suite, consisting of a master bedroom, huge living room and a smaller bedroom, were downright elegant.

On the floor was stretched a dark green rug with elaborately woven pictures of black bears lumbering along the borders. A huge poster bed made out of massive, rough-cut logs dominated the center of the room.

Kylie flipped off her shoes and bent down to peel off her socks. Grinning, she sunk her toes into the rug's softness. Heaven, pure unadulterated heaven.

Curious, she yanked back the fluffy down comforter and checked out the flannel sheets. She flattened her hand against the sheets testing the feather bedding beneath. Her fingers sank down a good five inches. Perfect. Maybe she'd actually get a good night's sleep. Surely such luxury had the capacity to stave off bad dreams.

She walked back out into the sitting area. Plush chairs, an oversize ottoman and a couch with woven cloth in rich earth tones sat next to white pine twig furniture. A slate-topped coffee table drew the area together, and a fieldstone fireplace threw out a blazing heat.

In one corner, stood a cherry oak bar. A collection of high-end liquor and elegantly cut crystal glasses lined the shelves in front of the etched mirror behind the bar.

Curious, she rounded the end of the bar and inspected the provisions in the small bar fridge. Enough expensive snack food to sustain a person for a month. No need to go hungry while enjoying all the comforts of home, or in her case, all the comforts she didn't experience at home.

Straightening up, she wandered over to the bearskin rug stretching the length of the hearth. Another grin tugged at the corners of her mouth. But this one definitely had a bit more of a playful feel to it. What Adirondack room would be complete without a bearskin rug?

Beneath her feet, the rug was thick and soft with a massive head at one end, the jaws open to display a dazzling array of sharp white teeth.

She bent down and touched one. The real McCoy. Amazing. She wondered if the maids were instructed to individually brush the teeth to keep them so white. She'd have to ask Sara tomorrow.

The sight of the rug and the fireplace amused her. There was only one thing any red-blooded American woman thought of when they saw that combination, and that was a romantic spot for making love. Too bad hers was going to go to waste.

Of course, if she had her druthers, it wouldn't go to waste. She knew exactly who she'd have stretched out on that rug if she could have her wish. One Michael Emerson, that's who.

Just the thought of the warm firelight touching his long, lean torso, showcasing the flat muscles of his abdomen and lower belly, was enough to send a shiver of unrestrained anticipation straight down to where it counted.

Apparently she was going to have to skip the hot bath she'd contemplated taking and go right for the needle-cold shower. If not, she was fairly certain sleep would be impossible tonight.

Or if she did sleep, she had a feeling her dreams would end up filled with thoughts of a particular adrenaline junkie's assault on her defenses while they lounged decadently on the thick bearskin rug.

She shook herself. For pity's sake, a simple fire in the hearth, a bearskin rug on the floor and she was reduced to this. Obviously once she got back home she was going to need to find some acceptable outlets for all this pent up sexual tension. Either that or attack Michael Emerson next time she met up with him.

A light knock on the suite door startled her out of self-indulgent fantasies.

Kylie crossed the room, a tiny quiver of caution rising in her belly. "Who's there?"

"Michael."

She undid the chain and slid back the lock. With a steadying breath she opened the door a crack.

Michael stood in the hall. All six foot three inches of him filled the doorway. There was a smile on his lips, something probably meant to be casual but which came across entirely too sexy.

Her mouth went dry and her cheeks reddened. Damn!

How was it that he always seemed to know when she was thinking about him? The man was uncanny with his timing.

"I'm glad to see you're taking precautions."

"A girl can never be too cautious." Especially when she was having crazy thoughts about the very man who now stood directly in front of her.

He had changed out of ski clothes, his lean hips and muscular thighs covered in worn jeans in a way that sent her heart into overdrive.

His shirt, a soft chambray blue that picked up the brilliant color of his eyes, was untucked and unbuttoned halfway, as if he'd been getting undressed, thought of her and decided to stop by for a chance encounter.

Her cheeks burned a little hotter. Oh brother, what made her think that he might give her a thought while getting ready for bed? Get a grip, Kylie!

"You going to be okay in here?" His voice, deep and slightly rough, like ultrafine sandpaper whisked along the column of her spine, sending a wild chill through her traitorous body.

How did one fight sensations like that? She had no defenses to work with whenever he was around. He seemed able to reduce her to a bundle of nerve endings with a single glance.

She gave him a neutral smile, trying her own nonchalance. "The room's magnificent. I couldn't ask for anything nicer. I really appreciate you arranging for me to have it."

He nodded, his expression anything but neutral. Heat, hot and smoldering, seemed to rise up off his frame, fanning her body and making the flames that scorched her insides burn like wildfire.

Kylie wondered if the room had air-conditioning.

A heavy silence settled between them.

Restless, she shifted from one foot to the other. He was standing too close. She could reach out and touch him.

Not that she needed to or anything. Her fingertips weren't itching to trace the tanned skin of his neck and smooth upper chest down the unbuttoned line of his shirt. No siree, that wasn't anything she was thinking about at all.

She chomped down on the inside of her cheek. *Get real, Kylie. That was exactly what you were thinking.*

Time to put a stop to this nonsense. She grabbed the doorknob. "Well, thanks for checking in on me, but I'm beat. I'm going to take a warm bath—" *Or a cold shower if my thoughts continue in the direction they seemed to be going.* "And then I'm going to turn in. It's been a long day."

He didn't move and she didn't have the courage to slam the door in his face.

"We need to talk."

Talking wasn't exactly what was on her mind. Her thoughts were running more along the line of bear rugs and naked bodies, but what the hell, if he wanted to talk, who was she to disagree?

Against her better judgment, she stepped back and allowed him to come in.

Immediately nervous, she moved to the bar. "Would you like a glass of wine? A beer? A—" Her voice sounded rushed, breathless.

But he interrupted smoothly, "How about a glass of Merlot?"

Frantic, she searched the shelves. Merlot. Where's the Merlot? There, on the second shelf.

Grabbing a bottle of Kendall Jackson as if it were a lifeline, she yanked open a drawer and fumbled around for a corkscrew.

Out of the corner of her eye, she saw him move to sit on the couch. He stretched his legs out in front of him and folded his hands behind his head. He had the look of a man settling in for the evening. This was not a good sign, not with her raging hormones kicking up an internal fuss.

She stabbed the corkscrew into the top of the bottle and turned. What she needed to do was get him out of her room as quickly as possible. The memory of his hands touching her, caressing her in the stairwell less than an hour ago was still too fresh. Too intimately demanding.

He watched her in studied silence as she pulled out the cork and poured them both a glass. It took all her inner strength to keep the bottle from rattling against the rim of the crystal.

For a moment, she considered grabbing an ice cube out of the freezer and running it along the surface of her hot skin. But she refrained, taking a calming breath

Damn him and his easy composure. Wasn't he in the least affected by the heat simmering between them? She checked him out from beneath slightly lowered lashes.

Nope, calm as the proverbial cucumber. All the more reason she needed to hustle him out of her room. She was still reeling from her encounter with Andrea and she didn't need the added distraction of Michael.

Sex and fear didn't mix. They led to mistakes. And neither of them needed to make a mistake. A mistake that would result in regrets.

She walked over to him and held out the glass. His fingers brushed hers, and her body reacted, a sharp pang of something wild, deep in her belly and lower.

She stepped back and dropped onto the hearth. The coolness of the stone beneath her legs was comforting.

She drew her legs close. Protective. Guarded.

She sipped the wine and watched him over the rim of the crystal, letting him know without saying anything that he was the one who had wanted to *talk.*

But he waited, too, his gaze never leaving hers, his eyes intense. Provocative.

She swallowed another sip of wine, feeling it flow through her veins, heating her blood even more. She quickly set the glass aside. What she didn't need was to get any warmer. The flames of the fire heated her spine and lower back. Another few seconds and she was going to ignite into her own personal bonfire.

"Ready to talk about what happened upstairs?"

"Not really."

She knew she was being difficult, uncooperative, but there wasn't any other way. She needed to close him out, keep him as far away as possible. Vulnerability made her cautious.

But for some reason, he didn't seem pick up on her signals. Or maybe he did pick up on them but chose to ignore them.

He stood up and moved closer, his body only inches from hers, so close his presence was suffocatingly warm. Sheltering and stirring all at the same time.

She didn't dare look up. Didn't dare make eye contact. If she did, she would lose the battle raging inside of her. A battle she had to win.

He reached down and touched her hair, his fingers running through the loose strands. Every nerve, on high alert since he'd entered the room, tightened and vibrated like an overstrung violin.

Unable to resist his pull, she turned her head, burying her lips against the callused hardness of his palm. She inhaled. He smelled of pine and wood and something totally male. Sharp and totally desirable.

His fingers, strong and quick, slid down the side of her face and cupped her chin. He lowered himself down, the muscles of his thighs imprisoning hers. She was trapped and nothing could have felt more right. More fitting.

"I—I think it would be better if you left," she protested.

"I think not."

She tried again. "This isn't okay."

He leaned in and pressed his lips to her ear, his hand sliding around and settling at the nape of her neck. "It's more than okay. It's perfection."

Her insides turned to liquid, melting at a temperature that seemed unbearable. At that moment, she wanted him so badly she thought she might self-destruct, her desire so burning, so outrageous, she felt as though she might disappear in a flash of wildfire.

But even as her insides turned to molten honey, a tiny kernel of doubt gnawed at the edges of her passion, making her hold back. Michael seemed to sense her guardedness and he tilted his head back, his intense gaze seeming to delve deep inside her, caressing her insides the same way his clever hands touched the sensitive skin at the back of her neck.

"A part of you still believes that I had something to do with the murders, right?"

There was no condemnation or anger to his words. Just a simple statement. Matter of fact.

It was as if he could see into her head, read her mind. And that scared her more than the thought that he really could somehow be connected to the murders. Scared her because it meant he'd gotten to her. Reached a part of her she thought she'd successfully hidden.

She lowered her eyes, as if looking away could shield the intensity of her feelings for him, the emotional turmoil raging inside her. But Michael was unwilling to accept that. He reached out and lifted her head, forcing her to meet his eyes again. "It's okay. Believe me, I've battled my own doubts."

"Really?"

He nodded, the intensity of his gaze dipping deeper, skimming along the edges of her soul. "But I've put those doubts to rest. There's no way I would ever hurt those women. I cared about each of them."

And somehow at that moment, just as he seemed able to reach out and touch her deepest thoughts and emotions, Kylie felt him open to her. She could see inside him and she knew the truth. There was no way Michael was responsible for the murders. She wasn't sure how she knew, but in a single instant, every fiber of her being screamed at her to trust her intuition. To trust in his innocence.

She leaned forward, pressing her lips to his, tasting him. Pure and sweet. He pulled her to him and slipped his arms around her, easing her to the floor.

The soft fur of the rug tickled the back of her neck, a strangely sensuous contrast to the hard unflinching body that settled over her.

He tugged at the hem of her shirt and his fingers slid over her bare skin with slow, sensuous strokes that made her whimper.

He bent his head and touched the tip of his tongue to the center of her belly. Air hissed from between her teeth and she lifted up to meet his clever mouth, never wanting the moment to end.

He unsnapped her jeans and peeled them off; his hands, rough and demanding, traveled the length of her body. She wanted him against her. Craved the touch of his skin against hers. Skin to skin. Body to aching body.

Desperate, she fumbled with the buttons of his shirt, yanking the hem from his jeans then pushing his jeans downward and reaching out to caress the smooth, hard muscles of his abdomen and lower.

Everything inside her was ready, all her senses awake and crying out. He rose up over her and drove into her. Strong. Powerful. She cried out once and then lifted her head to nip his shoulder, tasting him, teasing him. Savoring the essence of him.

Heat rose off him like a sultry summer's night, his movements forceful and electrifying. She moved with him, body to body, heartbeat to heartbeat, riding the crest until they reached the peak and fell together.

Her final thought as he pulled her closer, holding her pressed against him, was that perhaps not all battles were meant to be won. Some were worth losing.

"THAT WAS NICE." Her breath came in short, little pants and warmed his shoulder with pure sweetness.

"More than nice."

He propped his head up and grinned down at her, marveling at the halo of her dark, fragrant hair spread out across the rug, her eyelashes lifting to reveal eyes clouded with clear, sweet passion.

He reached out and ran the tip of one finger over her left breast and down the length of her body to her taut belly. He circled along the rim of her navel, loving how her skin fluttered and jumped beneath his touch. "You ready to tell me now what happened earlier?"

She gave a shaky laugh and squirmed beneath his touch. "Do you always resort to such exquisite torture to make your victims talk?"

"I only use this particular technique on special victims." He bent his head and trailed his tongue over the same path, pausing to add, "So talk. Tell me what happened."

"I saw Andrea again."

He lifted his head. "You mean you were having that dream again?"

She turned up on her side, her face troubled. "No, not a dream. It was her. She was standing in that room. The room we found the maid in. What is it about that room that is so important?"

His hand slid up over her belly to stroke the smooth, gentle glide of her hip. Her leg whispered against his as she moved to wrap it around him.

"I don't know."

"It has something to do with what's been is going on. I saw Andrea at that very window when we first arrived. Remember?"

He nodded.

"But this time she asked me to help her."

"She spoke?" It was hard for him to keep the disbelief out of his voice.

"No, not exactly. She wrote it."

"Wrote it how?

She looked slightly chagrined. "It was as if she breathed on the glass and then wrote in the mist. You know, like you do when you're a kid?"

"What was written on the window?"

"That she wanted me to find the *note*."

He settled back onto his elbow and stared down at her. Was she really expecting him to buy all of this? A child killed long ago suddenly appearing? Mysterious writing on windows?

It was little too whacked out for him. But then he had to admit that some pretty strange things had been happening in his life lately, and Kylie didn't strike him as an overly emotional woman prone to hysterical ranting. What if what she was saying was true? What if it was a clue to what was happening?

"What do you think the note is about?"

Kylie's top teeth chewed her bottom lip. Her frustration was obvious. "If I knew the answer to that, this whole case would be solved, and you'd be in the clear."

"So how do we figure out what she's referring to?"

"Good question. All I can think is that it has to be something to do with Andrea and that final summer we were all together."

She sat up and grabbed his shirt and pulled it on. A pang of disappointment crept over him. He liked drinking in her sleek nakedness.

"Why is that the only explanation?"

"Because there would be no other reason for Andrea's

ghost to appear. Her being here means that she is somehow involved."

"In what way?"

"Andrea's death has to be connected to the death of the other women."

Michael folded his hands behind his head and stared up at the ceiling, trying to consider what she proposed. Finally he shook his head. "It doesn't make sense, Kylie. The women were murdered. Andrea's death was an accident, not a murder."

Kylie scrambled to a sitting position, crossing her legs and leaning forward in excitement. "True. But what if her accident is somehow related to the reason the women are being murdered? What if the note she wants me to find tells us something about the identity of the murderer?"

"That would be great. Any chance she gave you a clue as to where to find this note?"

Kylie shook her head and her shoulders slumped a little, signaling the slight waning of her excitement. "I remember sitting around the campfire with the others when Gracie screamed. I reached the gorge just as Andrea disappeared beneath the waves.

A familiar pang of guilt flickered across her face, and he knew without asking that she was thinking of her failure to jump in after Andrea.

"You couldn't have rescued her, Kylie."

"We'll never know, will we?" She seemed to push aside the guilt, her expression hardening. "Do you remember where you were when the accident happened?"

He reached beneath the hem of her shirt and rested his hand on the inside curve of her leg, savoring the warm smoothness of her skin, trying to impart a sense of comfort.

"Reggie and I had just arrived. We'd gone into town to pick up supplies and a few of the local girls who had called earlier to say they wanted to come out to the party."

Kylie frowned.

"What?"

"That's not how I remember things. That night when Gracie came to tell me that she had to take care of Andrea, she told me that Nikki was supposed to meet up with you. She was mad that Nikki had dumped Andrea on us because we had plans to crash the party."

He shook his head. "She's mistaken. I was with Reggie."

"Strange."

"Why strange?"

"Because tonight when I talked with Gracie she seemed really angry with you. She feels that somehow you're responsible not only for her father dying, but for Andrea's death, too."

She lifted a hand to caress his cheek, her eyes questioning him, begging him to remember.

A stab of his own guilt shot through him and he nodded. "She's right about her father. I should have never taken him on that climb. I didn't see that he was bound and determined to prove something to himself. He took too many risks and I couldn't get through to him—convince him to slow down."

"I'm sorry. For the both of you." She leaned forward and laid her head against his shoulder, a tender gesture meant to lessen the blame he heaped upon himself. The two of them were carrying enough guilt to float an army. They needed to somehow get past it.

"I should have handled things differently."

She lifted her head and smiled. "A wise man once told me that it doesn't help to lay a lot of *should'ves* and *could'ves* on yourself."

He smiled. "How did I know those words would come back to haunt me?"

"Like I said, wise man."

"I can understand Gracie holding me responsible for her dad's accident, but not Andrea's."

Kylie tilted her head back. "She said that if you hadn't arranged to be with Nikki that night, Andrea would have never fallen off that cliff."

"But that's not what happened. I never even saw Nikki until after the police arrived."

"You weren't with her that night?"

He took her by the shoulders and met her gaze. "Nikki and I have always been friends, but even back then we were never intimately involved. Not ever."

"So, who was with Nikki that night? I know she was going off to meet someone."

"She had a date with Steven."

Kylie straightened up, surprise widening her eyes. "Steven?"

"On the afternoon before Andrea died, Steven told me that he'd finally gotten up the courage to ask Nikki out. He'd been carrying a torch for her for quite a while. He told me that he'd written her a note—" His voice trailed off as he considered what he'd just said.

Next to him, Kylie grabbed his arm, her fingers tightening with excitement. "Steven wrote her a *note?* What kind of note?"

"According to what he said to me, he'd written her a note telling her to meet him at the hotel that night." He raked a hand through his hair. "Damn, I'd forgotten all about that. Do you think that's the note?"

"I don't know. But we need to find out." She glanced at the clock on the mantle. "Darn it! It's 2:00 a.m. Too late to go ask him now."

Michael allowed his hand on her knee to rove higher. "Hmmm, guess we're just going to have to think of something to do until we can bother poor Steven."

She laughed, the sound throaty and infinitely sexy. A thrill of hot desire shot through him as she scooted across the fur rug and slid onto his lap, wrapping her legs around his waist as she rose up and over him.

"Guess we'll just have to think of something indecent to do until a decent hour arrives," she whispered as she leaned forward to run her tongue along his bottom lip before slipping inside to taste him.

Michael pulled her closer, acutely aware that he couldn't have agreed more. Passing the time had never been so inviting. So perfect.

KYLIE STRETCHED, a grin of satisfaction tugging at the corners of her mouth.

No need to open her eyes to recognize the feeling of pure, unadulterated contentment. The sensation infused every single cell of her body.

Nothing like wild sex to make a woman truly believe things were on the upswing in her life. And if her current level of contentment was any indication, she figured her life was about to shoot into the stratosphere.

She felt boneless. Totally weightless and miraculously complete.

At some point during the night, they had stumbled into the bedroom to give the bed a turn, and Kylie wasn't sure whether the bear rug or the huge Adirondack bed was her favorite place to play. Each held their own degree of sensuous delight. She was glad she wouldn't be forced to choose.

Rolling over, she reached for Michael. His spot beside her was empty. She ran her fingers over the sheets. Still warm. He couldn't have been gone long.

She sat up and looked around. There were no sounds from the bathroom and his clothes, previously strewn haphazardly across the floor were gone. He'd dressed quietly and left while she was still asleep.

The suite was dark. Quiet.

She grabbed the clock off the bedside table and clicked on the night-light. Early. Only 4:00 a.m.

With a stab of disappointment, she wondered if Michael had gone back to his room, leaving her to finish out the night alone.

Although she appreciated his thoughtfulness of not waking her up, she would have liked to have been given the opportunity to tell him it was fine with her if he stayed the night.

She grinned. Heck, with the way he made her body hum, she figured she could be persuaded to let him stay each and every night.

Perhaps she'd tiptoe across the hall and return the favor. A jab of delightful wickedness shot through her at the thought. Good. Time for her to let go some. Sleeping alone, even in an elegant suite of rooms, was not all it was cracked up to be.

She slid out of bed and grabbed her robe, knotting it around her waist as she stuck a bare foot under the bed and felt around for her slippers. She slid her feet into them and padded out into the living room.

The fire had burned down to glowing ash. A coolness filled the room. She reached for the knob, surprised to find the door unlocked. Strange. Why would he leave the door unlocked with all that had been going on?

Behind her, a small thud came from the smaller bedroom.

She paused, her hand on the door. "Michael?"

A heavy silence hung over the suite.

Slowly she made her way across the room to the other adjoining room. The door stood slightly ajar.

"Michael, is that you?"

She pushed open the door and stepped inside.

The room was dark, filled with shadows.

A strange shiver of fear crept up her spine, settling into the back of her neck.

Something was wrong. Terribly wrong.

She turned to leave, to get out, but the door slammed shut with a bang. The room was plunged into total darkness.

A shadow flitted off to the right. She jumped.

"W-who's there?"

Cold air brushed the back of her neck.

She fumbled for the doorknob and something hard hit the middle of her back. She cried out as pain shot across her shoulders and ran down her arms. Her fingers went numb.

Another blow hit and she stumbled, falling forward. She threw out her hands to catch herself.

The floor came up to meet her. She scrambled to get up, but her legs wouldn't move.

She tried to roll over but something struck the back of her head. Light sparks burst behind her eyelids.

She shook her head, desperately trying to stay conscious. But a dark pit yawned, pulling her in, dragging her down.

As darkness folded around her, two hands clamped around her neck and squeezed. She couldn't breathe. Couldn't scream.

She let go and disappeared over the edge into the pit.

Chapter Eleven

"Can you open your eyes?"

The voice, soft and comforting, seemed to come from a great distance away, but Kylie struggled to obey.

Her eyelids seemed heavy, weighted down. They opened slowly.

Sara Dell stood over her, her lined face tense and concerned.

"W-where am I?" she asked, her hand going up to explore the tender spot at the back of her head. It felt as though a tiny gnome with a sledgehammer the size of a construction jackhammer had taken up permanent residence in her brain.

"You're in your room."

Beneath her, the bed which such a short time ago had been so comfortable, now seemed like a board, pressing in on her sore, aching body.

She winced as her fingers touched the bandage covering a spot at the back of her head. Her throat hurt almost as much as her head, and her voice sounded hoarse. She dropped her hand to rub her neck.

"What happened?" she croaked.

"You were attacked, sweetie." Sara reached behind her to adjust the pillows. "Gracie heard you scream."

From the end of the bed, Gracie touched her foot. "I found you unconscious on the floor." She glanced anxiously at Denner, who stood on the other side of the bed, and then back again. "Someone tried to strangle you."

Well, that explained the pain in her throat but not who had done it.

Sara continued to rearrange the pillows sending a totally new stab of pain shooting through the top of Kylie's head. She grabbed Sara's wrist to stop her from fussing. "Who hit me?"

Detective Denner scowled. "Who the hell do you think?"

"I wouldn't ask if I knew." Kylie tried to sit up, but the room tilted crazily and she was forced to drop her head back onto the pillow. "I couldn't see anything. It was too dark. Whoever was in the room hit me from behind. The last thing I remember was blacking out."

"For the past three days I've been telling you that Emerson is a homicidal maniac. Now maybe you'll believe me."

Kylie sat bold upright, ignoring the wave of nausea that filled her stomach. "No! That's not possible. There's no way Michael was the one who attacked me."

Gracie moved to the head of the bed, sitting beside her. She gently pushed her back down. "You've got to rest. You were hit pretty hard."

Kylie's gaze sought her friend's. "Tell them they're wrong, Gracie. Tell them it wasn't Michael."

Gracie shook her head, her expression pained. "I'm sorry but it was Michael. I found him on top of you choking you from behind."

She smoothed back several strands of hair that caught against the side of Kylie's face, her hand cool against her damp cheek. "We're just lucky that he didn't see me. He had his back to the door. I grabbed a log from the firebox and hit him. Detective Denner heard us struggling and came to help. If he hadn't come, I don't know what would have happened."

"This can't be true."

Denner snorted in disgust. "I don't have time to listen to this." He headed for the door. "I've got to get Emerson downstairs. I'll talk to you when you smarten up and realize that Michael Emerson is the killer I've said he is."

As he stormed out of the room, Kylie closed her eyes. There was no way that the things Denner and Gracie said about Michael could be true. She had trusted him, believed him when he said he wasn't responsible for the murders.

Somehow she needed to clear her head and figure out what had happened. Her trust in Michael couldn't have been wrong.

Could it?

SEVERAL HOURS LATER, Michael settled back against the chair and slipped his left index finger under the handcuff's metal ring, rubbing the tender spot on his inside right wrist.

Denner had taken real pleasure in marching him downstairs and snapping the cuffs on him, securing the other end to the exposed heating pipe next to the easy chair.

Unless someone had the foresight to bring him a hacksaw, Michael was fairly certain he was stuck in the library for the duration of the storm. Not that he figured anyone would be doing that anytime soon. Something told him he deserved everything that had happened to him.

After making love to Kylie, he had left her sleeping to run down to the kitchen to get something to eat. Another headache had started and he had figured a little food might help stave off a full-fledged attack.

Last thing he remembered was standing in the kitchen making a ham-and-cheese sandwich and setting it on a tray to take back upstairs. Then everything went blank.

Later, when things came back in focus, he'd found himself sprawled spread-eagle on the floor of Kylie's room, an excruciating headache pounding him into total submission. His head still ached.

He had looked up to find Denner standing over him, his gun drawn. It wasn't until later that he'd learned he'd been found straddling Kylie, his hands wrapped around her neck.

He laid his head back against the cushion and stared at the ceiling. The molding along the edges of the room was beginning to peel. He made a mental note to tell Templer to get the new caretaker to make sure the room was repainted before the summer season. But as soon as the thought flashed through his brain, he dismissed it.

Molding. What the hell was wrong with him? He was worried about molding, and he had almost killed someone, choked her so hard he'd left bruises.

It was time he accepted facts. There was no room for any more doubts. The blackouts meant he was out of control. Totally out of control.

What he couldn't figure out was why had he tried to kill Kylie? Were his feelings for her and the other women somehow connected to a strange, uncontrollable urge to kill? How was he supposed to make sense out of any of this if he couldn't remember attacking her? Or any of the others.

Across the room the library door opened.

Kylie slipped in, a finger to her lips, motioning for him not to speak.

He watched as she carefully closed the door, using one hand to muffle the snick of the lock. He couldn't help but notice that she moved with studied slowness as if in pain. The bruised and reddened flesh encircling her slender neck told him that someone had indeed tried to choke her. The thought of anyone hurting her sent a charge of undeniable rage shooting through him.

"What are you doing here?" he asked, straightening up. "No one is supposed to be anywhere near me."

She shook her head, again motioned for him not to speak. She pressed an ear to the door and listened intently for several seconds.

Finally she straightened up and approached him. She eased herself onto the hassock next to him, wincing slightly as if every movement caused her pain.

She leaned in. "I can't stay long. If Denner finds me in here, he won't be happy." Her voice was hoarse. Rough.

"He's right to tell you to stay away. I'm dangerous."

She shook her head. "No, you're not."

He reached up, the cuffs biting into his wrists, but he ignored the pain. He gently traced the tender, bruised skin of her neck, a terrible sorrow eating at his heart. How could he have done that to her?

"I did that to you."

"No, you didn't. And that's why I'm here." She placed a cool palm over his hand, her touch forgiving. Gentle. "There's another explanation. There has to be."

He slipped his hand out from under hers. Seeing her was

hard enough. Touching her was too hard. He needed to keep his distance. That was the only way he could be sure she was safe.

"No. Sitting here has made me realize that I did it. There isn't any other explanation. I haven't been completely honest. I haven't been able to tell you about the blank periods."

Her dark brows drew together. "What blank periods?"

"I've been getting headaches. Bad headaches."

"I know, you told me. But that's pretty common after a severe concussion. It takes time to recover. But your symptoms are getting worse. That tells me that something is seriously wrong."

"And that's why I'm saying that I could be the killer. I haven't been completely honest. Sometimes when I get the headaches, I can't remember things. It's like things go completely blank for periods of time and the periods are getting longer."

She captured his face between her hands, her gaze fixed on his. "Listen to me, you're *not* a murderer. The symptoms you're describing are serious, but they don't mean you killed anyone. Or that you tried to kill me."

Her voice was calm. Completely convincing. He almost believed her. Almost but not quite. It was impossible to ignore the angry welts bruising her neck. They were too visible. Too much of a reality check. He had done that to her.

She seemed to sense his disbelief. "We need to get you to a doctor, Michael. Figure out what's going on. But first we have to find out who is setting you up."

"How can you believe that I'm not responsible after what I did to you?"

"Because I know it wasn't you who attacked me. You

don't have it in you. Someone else knocked me unconscious and then blamed you."

She stared into his eyes, and the trust swimming in their depths was so deep it seemed to fill him. Her hands slid around his neck and she pulled him to her. He could feel the steady beat of her heart. Reassuring. Life-giving.

"How do you know?"

"I just know." She sat back but stayed in contact with him by slipping her hand through his. A small smile played with her exquisite mouth. "In case you've forgotten, I had a chance to smell you up close. Whoever attacked me didn't smell in the least like you."

"I'd like to believe you know what you're talking about, but you're forgetting that I was found on top of you, actually trying to choke you. Gracie had to hit me over the head just to get me off."

"I'm not buying what Gracie said."

He opened his mouth again, but she put a finger across his lips, cutting him off. "Don't argue," she warned. "We don't have a lot of time. Tell me the name of the hospital where Gracie's father put her after Andrea's death."

"Why?"

"Because Gracie isn't telling the whole truth. She's hiding something."

"You can't be thinking that Gracie killed those women." He forced a laugh. "Come on, Kylie. Gracie can't get out of her own way. She doesn't have the strength to lower a body down into a ravine and then climb down there to drive in an ice screw and leave the body there." He shook his head. "Besides, what reason would she have to kill those women?"

"I'm not sure yet, but trust me when I say that Gracie is a lot stronger and more agile than she looks. It's part of the reason I suspect she's up to something. She's tried to hide the fact that she's as strong as she is. Plus, it's pretty clear that she harbors a great deal of resentment toward you."

She tugged on the sleeve of his shirt. "So, do you remember the hospital she was in or not?"

"Some place in Vermont. Nikki said the name of the place last night." He frowned, struggling to recall the name. "Bratten something or other."

Her eyes lit up. "Brattenhurst Retreat! Right?"

"Yeah, that's it. What are you going to do?"

She leaned across and kissed him, pressing her lips tight against his mouth for a brief, dizzying moment. He reached out with one hand to pull her closer but she laughed and dodged him.

"Gotta go. I need to make a phone call." She walked to the door, slowly, opening it a crack and peeking out. Before she slipped out into the hall, she blew him a quick kiss over one shoulder. "Be good."

He lifted his restrained hand as far as the handcuffs allowed. "How can I be anything but?"

She disappeared as quickly as she'd come, leaving him to wonder what she was up to.

"THE PHONES are still out," Templer warned Kylie as she picked up the receiver in the main lobby. "Even with the storm almost over, I don't see them getting fixed for several more days."

Kylie nodded and replaced the dead receiver in the cradle. She had to find a way to get the information she needed. "Any chance a cell phone might work?"

Templer glanced at the windows. "The storm calmed down significantly. It might be worth a try." He gave her a condescending look. "Do you own one?"

Kylie couldn't help but smile. The man was so predictable. If he had one she was pretty sure he wouldn't loan it to her. Probably thought she'd run up a bill and then skip town without paying. The possibility of putting the snooty manager's nose out of joint made her seriously tempted to do exactly that, but she decided not to tweak him any more than necessary. They were still confined to the hotel. No sense in making an enemy hate her even more.

"I'm sure someone has one I can borrow."

Across the room, Leslie looked up from the magazine she was leafing through. "You can use mine," she offered. "It's in my leather bag next to the front door. Check the front pocket."

She flipped the magazine onto the coffee table. "I don't know about you, but I'm already packed and ready to go. As soon as the police arrive, I'm out of here!"

Kylie nodded her thanks and quickly retrieved the woman's cell phone.

"Who are you calling?" Gracie said, walking in from the dining room.

"Oh, I thought I'd try to get a hold of my neighbor. Need to make sure everything is okay in my apartment. Let her know that I won't be home for a few more days."

Gracie nodded, but she watched carefully as Kylie tucked the phone in her back pocket.

"Uh, I left my address book upstairs so I think I'll make the call from there," Kylie said. "I'll be back down in a little bit."

She climbed the stairs slowly, but once she made the turn on the landing, she raced the rest of the way up. Making the call in private was critical.

Practically panting, she closed and locked her door, trying the phone on the way to the bedroom. Eureka! Her call went through. They were finally reconnected to the outside world.

A few minutes later, she located the number of the Brattenhurst Retreat outside Essex, Vermont.

She sucked in a calming breath as she punched in the number and waited for the call to go through. A few seconds later, she was connected with the hospital's switchboard. She asked for the admissions office.

"Good afternoon, Brattenhurst Retreat," a pleasant, slightly musical voice said in greeting.

"Hello. I'm hoping that you can help me with some information," she said.

"I'll try. What information were you seeking?" the woman asked.

"I know that confidentiality prevents you from giving me any information about a particular patient, but I was wondering if you could help me understand the different types of programs you run there at Brattenhurst."

"Certainly. General information about our facility is always available. Do you have any particular program you'd be interested in hearing about or would you prefer I mail you one of our lovely brochures. It outlines very clearly our full list of services."

"Uh, no." Kylie sat on the edge of the bed, shifting the phone to her other ear. "I'm sure you can provide everything I need over the phone. I'm particularly interested in the type of self-esteem, skill-building programs you run for in-patients. You know, the kind of program that incorporates physical fitness and adventure sports into treatment?"

"Of course. We have one particular program, *The Life Affirming Whole Health Program,* that would fit that description. It's our most popular program actually. Considered very innovative by the therapeutic community." The woman's voice warmed to the subject of promoting her employer. "Patients are given the opportunity to work with a personal trainer to get into the best physical shape of their lives. We operate under the philosophy of—"

"I don't mean to interrupt, but could you tell me a bit about the different kinds of activities your patients participate in?"

"Oh, the sky's the limit. Some of the most popular activities are white-water rafting, rock climbing, ice climbing, cross-country skiing. You name it, we do it!"

Kylie's heart beat faster. Bingo! She'd hit the jackpot.

"How long has the program been in existence?"

"I'd have to check with one of our staff, but I'd say this program started about six years ago." She paused a moment and then asked, "Were you interested in coming to Brattenhurst yourself or is this inquiry on behalf of a family member?"

"Oh, no one in particular. Just curious." She was eager to end the conversation. "Thanks ever so much for your help. If I decide on Brattenhurst, I'll be sure to call."

"Wouldn't you like me to mail you one of our lovely—"

Kylie clicked off, dropping the cell phone onto the bed. She sat there in the middle of the bed, digesting what she'd learned.

According to Nikki's tirade the other night, Gracie had been to Brattenhurst recently. No doubt she'd participated in the Whole Health Program at the hospital, most likely more than once. That meant that she was clearly capable of physically overpowering any of the women killed in addition to climbing down an ice fall. With Gracie's strange sense of rage directed at Michael it seemed more than possible that she was the killer.

Now all she needed to do was find the evidence and convince Denner that Michael was not the killer he sought. As she considered what she would do next, the door to the suite crashed open and Nikki strolled through.

"Have you seen Gracie?" she asked, not in the least disturbed that she'd entered without knocking.

Kylie got up off the bed and walked into the outer room. "I haven't seen her. Did you check the gym?"

"I've checked everywhere. It's like she vanished off the face of the earth."

She hid the sense of dread that shot through her. If Gracie took off and they couldn't locate her, then her plans to clear Michael would be severely hampered. She needed Gracie to prove her case.

"I haven't seen her since Denner took Michael into custody, locking him up in the library like he was a common criminal." Nikki walked over to the window and peered out. "What's wrong with everyone? First Michael goes crazy, choking you. And now Gracie is gone."

"She's probably around somewhere. I'll help you look."

Damn right she'd help her look. She needed Gracie found. Michael's freedom depended on it.

"I'll check this floor. You go find some of the others and start searching the other floors," she instructed.

Nikki nodded and headed off to round up the others.

Chapter Twelve

As she started to leave the suite, Kylie stopped.

She turned and stared at the door to the smaller bedroom, the room Gracie and Nikki had slept in as children.

Her heart beat faster and a line of sweat broke out between her shoulder blades. Memories of her struggle last night flashed through her mind.

She stepped toward the bedroom and then froze.

If Gracie was the killer, was it possible that she'd been the one who was inside the smaller bedroom last night? Was she the one who had attacked her?

She shook her head. How could that be? Gracie had said she'd never set foot in the suite again.

But if she was the killer, it made perfect sense that she was the one Kylie had heard moving around in the room last night. Why? What could have drawn her to enter the room again?

She retraced her steps to the room. Her hands tingled with anticipation as she pushed open the door. The drapes partially open, faint afternoon light filled the room.

The room was empty.

She stepped into the center and made a full circle, surveying the entire room.

Nothing looked disturbed. The beds were made. The two small dressers and nightstands clear with the exception of a thin film of dust. Maid service had been slightly remiss.

She walked to the closet and opened the door.

Expensive velvet-covered hangers hung empty on the two racks running the length of the walk-in closet.

She turned around again.

What had Gracie wanted in here?

Her eye fell upon the pictures hanging on the walls of the room. Three in all. Each a magnificent photo of the Adirondacks. But it was the photo over one of the beds that caught her attention.

It was of the gorge. A photo that caught the cliffs at sunset, the glow of the setting sun bouncing off the sides of the stone walls and reflecting back a brilliant glow of blood-red.

The picture was breathtakingly beautiful and frightening all at the same time, capturing the sheer dizzying drop of the cliff walls and the wild race of the violent river below.

Kylie cocked her head. From where she stood, the picture seemed to dip a fraction of an inch to the right, as if someone had knocked the frame.

Stepping over to the bed, she lifted the frame off the hook and turned it over. There tucked into the plain brown backing of the photo was a folded piece of white paper.

Her heart ticked up a beat. She pulled it out and sat on the edge of the bed. The paper was worn and creased, as if it had been folded and refolded numerous times.

Carefully she opened it and read:

Nikki,
Meet me in Room 416 tonight at 6:00 p.m.
Don't be late!

The name *Michael* was neatly signed at the bottom of the note.

Kylie frowned. This had to be the note Andrea had wanted her to find. But Michael had sworn he hadn't been with Nikki that night, that he hadn't written her a note asking for a rendezvous.

He'd insisted that Steven was the one who had been in love with Nikki and had written the note asking to meet. So what was Michael's name doing at the bottom?

And then, as she studied the note she understood.

Refolding the note, she ran for the stairs.

MICHAEL SAT at the kitchen table awkwardly holding a soup spoon in his hand. It wasn't easy to eat with handcuffs on, even with his hands cuffed in front.

Denner had brought him into the kitchen a few minutes earlier, instructing him to hurry up and eat.

As she had put food on the table, Sara shot a sympathetic glance in his direction, but she made no attempt to engage him in conversation. The two maintenance men, Tommy and Del, occupied the seats on his right. They kept their heads down, their attention on their meal. Steven and Leslie sat across from him. None of them made eye contact.

It didn't take a genius to know that all of them were

considering the possibility that he was the killer. The only one who seemed willing to believe he might not be guilty was Kylie. Even he wasn't totally convinced he hadn't killed someone.

He sipped the thick broth and listlessly chewed a few carrots. He wasn't in the least bit hungry, but since Denner hadn't brought him anything for lunch, Michael figured he needed to eat. No matter that the food made him nauseous and his head pounded relentlessly. He needed to keep his strength up.

He glanced toward the door, wondering where Kylie and the others were. The hotel had seemed as quiet as a tomb for the last few hours or so.

"Any word from town?" he asked.

Denner looked up from his four-day-old newspaper and regarded him with a sour look. "Got a call through to Lieutenant Robbins earlier on my cell phone. He figures they'll be able to come out and pick you up tomorrow morning. The plows won't be able to get through tonight." He adjusted his glasses and went back to reading.

"Are you planning to make me spend the night handcuffed to the pipe in the library?"

"Can't think of a better place for you." Denner casually glanced over the top of the paper. "Maybe I'll be generous enough to push the couch over to the pipe—let you stretch out. Depends on my mood later this evening." He went back to reading.

The door swung open and Kylie burst into the kitchen. Everyone looked up.

"Gracie's missing. Have any of you seen her?"

"Saw her taking out a snowmobile about an hour ago," Del said, glancing up from slurping his soup. "Said she was going for a little ride."

"No one stopped her?" Kylie asked.

"Why would I? She said she wasn't going far. Probably had cabin fe—"

"What's wrong, Kylie?" Michael interrupted.

She held up a small scrap of paper. "I found this note upstairs. It's the note we've been looking for."

Denner scowled. "What note?"

Michael could see the indecision on Kylie's face. If she told Denner about the ghost sighting he wasn't going to take anything she had to tell him seriously. But how did she explain the note?

She leaned over the table, spreading the scrap of paper open. "Michael and I think the death of Gracie and Nikki's younger sister is connected to the murders. Remember the Crime Scene Investigators found a photo of Andrea Greenley in the maid's hand?"

"Yeah," Denner drew the comment out, his confusion apparent.

"Well, I think the maid found the picture in a photo album along with this note tucked into the back of the picture."

"So what? The note just says that Emerson wanted to meet up with Ms. Greenley—what, eleven years ago? What does that have to do with the current murders?"

"It doesn't mean anything to *us,* but to the killer it was proof that Michael convinced Nikki to meet him the night she was supposed to watch Andrea Greenley. The killer holds him responsible for Andrea's death. She believes that if Nikki hadn't left that night to go off to meet Michael, Andrea would still be alive."

Denner's expression was incredulous. "She? You think the killer is a woman?"

Kylie nodded. "It's Gracie Greenley."

Denner threw back his head and laughed. "Oh, lady, you're rich. You think Gracie Greenley has killed all these women?"

Kylie slipped into the chair next to Denner, her facial features intent, pleading. "Hear me out. Gracie isn't thinking rationally. She's always held Michael responsible for Andrea's death. And when her father died on a climb with him six months ago, she snapped. She believed Michael was to blame for her father's death, too. She couldn't handle it anymore. She had to make him pay."

Denner snorted. "And how exactly does that translate into her killing the women? If she wanted revenge, why didn't she just kill Emerson?"

"Because Gracie wanted Michael to pay. To suffer. And simply killing him would have been too easy."

Denner didn't look convinced.

"Don't you see? Gracie has been awash in guilt, drowning in it. She's lived in her own personal hell for so many years that she can't think straight. All she's ever wanted was to make Michael suffer the way she suffered." Kylie leaned forward, her voice urgent. "Gracie believed that the best way to make Michael pay for the death of her little sister and her father's fall was to force the people who cared about him to suspect him of murder. To fear him. To draw away from him in horror. She wanted them to reject him in the same way her family rejected her—ostracized her."

Michael sat back, understanding dawning. He knew that

the Greenley family had always held Gracie accountable for Andrea's death. No one had ever been able to convince them otherwise, and her father had been the one to reject his daughter the most.

Up until this moment, Michael had never truly appreciated the pain Gracie had endured, the anguish her family's rejection had caused her, Kylie's words explained a lot.

"But why the women?" Denner pressed.

"Because they were at the cliffs that night eleven years ago. They didn't play a role in Andrea's death, but in some warped way, Gracie still held them responsible. Not in the same way she's held Michael responsible, but she still hated them. Hated all of us for the role we played in Andrea's fall. Gracie believes that everyone who attended that party eleven years ago has to pay in some way."

Kylie sat back, one hand going to her throat. She swallowed hard and Michael could tell from the slight frown between her eyebrows that all this talking was straining her throat. But she wasn't done. "But ultimately, Gracie hated Michael the most. She saw him as the one who convinced Nikki to ditch Andrea for a romantic rendezvous at the lodge. In Gracie's mind, if Michael hadn't sent the note, then Andrea would still be alive today."

Steven set down his mug and reached across the table to pick up the note. "Michael didn't write this. I did."

Kylie nodded. "I know. Michael's already told me that you were the one who arranged to meet Nikki that night. What I don't understand is why you put Michael's name at the bottom."

Steven shrugged, his expression sheepish. "I was crazy for Nikki." He gave a short laugh. "Still am. But back when we were kids, I knew she'd never come if the note was from me."

He shot Michael an apologetic glance. "Sorry, buddy. I never meant for you to get the blame, but I figured that if I put my name at the bottom Nikki would never come to meet me."

"Did she?" Kylie asked.

"Yes, but she laughed at me. Told me that nothing would ever happen between us. I think she would have lit into me good for luring her there under false pretenses, but by then the whole hotel was in an uproar over Andrea's accident. We took off."

He refolded the note and handed it back to Kylie. "I never knew what happened to the note. I thought it had gotten lost."

"I think Gracie must have found it," Kylie said.

"Look, as nice as all of this is, it doesn't change a damn thing." Denner stood up and glanced at Michael. "You done?"

Kylie grabbed his arm. "But what about Gracie taking off? Doesn't it prove that she's guilty?"

"Not by a long shot." Denner brushed her aside and hooked a beefy hand through the crook of Michael's elbow. He led him out of the room. "You can tell your preposterous story to the State Police tomorrow. But until then, stay out of the library and away from Emerson."

Michael walked back to the library, feeling for all the world like the condemned man just denied a pardon from the warden. Kylie had tried her best but there was no convincing Denner of anything. Least of all his innocence.

It was going to be a long night.

SHE WAS DREAMING again.

Wind whipped across her face, warm and full of promise. She stepped out onto the edge of the cliff and her bare toes wrapped over the edge in anticipation.

She threw her arms up, embracing the feel of the setting sun on her arms and face. An eagle soared overhead, its wings extended, dipping and swaying on the crosswinds.

She tensed her muscles, gathering her strength and jumped. The world spun and twisted on its axis as she leaped outward into the canyon space.

For an instant, her body was weightless, totally free, and she yelled.

And then, she dropped. Air rushed against her ears and hammered her body. She fell, every bone in her body braced for the hit.

She plunged feetfirst into the waters below.

Waves, strong and wild, crashed and closed over her head. She sunk into the depths of the river, going down. Down into the toe-numbing coldness of the deepest part of the river.

She opened her eyes, bubbles danced and rose around her, encasing her body, tickling and pushing her back up.

And then she saw her. Andrea, her small body a few inches away, her eyes open, a soft, childish smile on her mouth.

Kylie held out her hand and Andrea took it, her tiny fingers grasping hers, somehow feeling warm and comforting in the coldness of the river water. They rose, side by side, headed for the surface.

Their heads bobbed above the waves, their mouths open to gasp in great lungfuls of air, and their laughter mixed and mingled. Andrea's arms tightened around her neck, her body, wet and slippery, clung to her as Kylie towed her ashore.

Overhead, the sun blazed hot and steamy, beating down on them and warming their chilled bodies as they climbed out of the river onto the rocks.

Andrea hugged her harder, whispering in her ear, "You came for me. You really came for me this time."

"Yes, this time I came back." Kylie wrapped her arms around the tiny body and gently stroked the small girl's wet hair.

She'd been there for Andrea. A sense of peace settled over her, telling her she hadn't left the little girl behind. She'd found the courage to do what she never thought she'd be able to do.

KYLIE WOKE with a start, a smile of such joy on her lips that she almost laughed aloud.

She had leaped out into the gorge, plunging into the cold clean water below.

She sat up and checked the time: 2:00 a.m.

Climbing out of bed, she moved to the window and pushed aside the drapes, staring out at the estate. For the first time in four days no snow was falling. She wondered if Gracie was okay. If she'd gotten safely into town or if she'd been lost somewhere out there in the snowstorm.

Overnight, the storm clouds had broken up and stars shone through the thin covering rushing overhead.

Moonlight spilled over the tops of the pines onto the front of the hotel. She was bathed in its silver rays.

She leaned on the sill and took in the stark beauty of the fresh snow in the moonlight.

Suddenly a cold breeze brushed the back of her nightgown, lifting the hem as if someone had touched her lower back.

She whirled around.

The room was dark, a shaft of moonlight streaming through the open curtain and spilling onto the floor. She exhaled, her breath white vapor. Her skin pebbled and a chill ran up the length of her exposed arms.

She was frozen. Waiting.

And the bluish light came, drifting in from the living room.

The translucent shape of a small child tiptoed into the room, her small frame disappearing and reappearing in the moonlight.

Andrea. She'd come one final time.

"What do you want?" she whispered softly. "What is it that you're trying to tell me?"

The small figure raised a hand and motioned for her to follow. She seemed to drift out of the room.

Kylie's heart pounded but her feet seemed unwilling to move.

Finally she forced one foot in front of the other, following the faint wavering figure. The suite door swung open as if on its own, and the ghost swept through, turning once to see that she was following.

Andrea headed down the hall to the stairs. She seemed to disappear, but when Kylie stepped onto the landing and headed down the final steps, she saw the child ahead of her, moving, floating across the lobby toward the library.

A terrible urgency swept through Kylie.

Michael. She was taking her to Michael.

Something was wrong.

She ran the length of the hall, her feet pounding against the floor, her breath rasping her throat.

The door to the library swung open and Andrea swept through. Kylie followed.

In the dim firelight, she saw Michael stretched out on the couch, his right arm latched securely to the heating pipe. His eyes were closed, unable to see the figure standing over him, her hand raised.

"Gracie, stop!" she yelled.

Gracie turned, her face contorted into a mask of rage. Her green eyes, usually so placid and soft, sparked a madness that defied description.

The knife in her hand glinted silver in the firelight. She dropped down onto the edge of the couch and pressed the blade to Michael's throat, a thin line of blood seeping down the side of the edge.

His eyelids snapped open, his expression confused for a moment until he realized who sat next to him. His gaze met Kylie's and she saw the concern for her in his eyes.

"Don't come any closer, Kylie." His eyes begged her to listen to him. To do as he asked.

"Yeah, don't press your luck, Kylie," Gracie said. "I didn't kill you the last time. But you won't get off so easily this go-round."

"So it was you who attacked me from behind." Kylie moved slowly, circling around the two of them, trying to get to the trophy wall and the framed articles.

There was no time to go for help. She needed to keep Gracie calm, her hand steady, or Michael was dead. She needed to convince her of Michael's innocence.

"Michael wasn't responsible for Andrea's death, Gracie."

"He was. If he hadn't enticed Nikki to meet him at the hotel she would have never asked me to watch Andrea." The thin line of blood gushed a little more as Gracie leaned on the blade. "Andrea wouldn't have wandered off. Wouldn't have disobeyed Nikki."

"You've got it all wrong. Michael didn't write the note."

"Don't try to trick me. I saw the note. It has his name at the bottom. He's to blame."

Kylie took out the note, unfolded it and stuck it up against the glass of one of the old articles written by Michael. "Come look, Gracie. Come see that the signatures don't match. Even when Michael was a kid he used the eagle to embellish his signature. No eagle. No sprawling signature."

Gracie glanced up, for the first time indecision flickering across her broad face. Kylie watched her right hand, hoping the knife blade would loosen, but it didn't. Michael didn't dare lift his head.

Frustrated, Kylie smacked her hand against the wall. "Come and look. What would it hurt to just look? It's not Michael's handwriting. Steven was the one who wrote the note. Ask Nikki. Nikki will tell you Michael didn't write it. Steven was the one who arranged to meet Nikki in room 416 that night."

Gracie's confusion deepened. "Nikki would say anything to protect Michael." Her eyes hardened. "You would, too. Women will do anything fo—"

The room was suddenly filled with heartrending sobs and Gracie stopped in midsentence.

"W-who's there?" she demanded, her voice trembling.

A bluish light filled one corner of the room and the tiny figure of Andrea appeared. Tears streamed down her face and she held up her hands to her sister.

"Andrea?" Gracie's face paled and she stood up, her eyes wide with wonderment. "Andrea, is that you? Is that really you?"

Beside her, Miçhael sat up and grabbed for the knife, wrestling it out of Gracie's hand.

Gracie let go, her body slumping to the floor.

Epilogue

Two Months Later

Spring had arrived early in the Adirondacks. The sweet smell of rain and budding trees filled the air over the gorge.

Kylie laid the small bunch of daisies on the rock beside her and pushed her baseball cap back on her head, staring up at the brilliant blue of the sky.

An eagle turned and soared overhead, its wings wide and magnificent.

"Beautiful, isn't he?"

She turned to see Michael coming up the path, moving slowly but steadily. She smiled, sweet desire rising up in her just at the sight of him.

God, she loved him. Couldn't get enough of him. It was as if he'd replaced something long gone inside her. Made her life more complete.

"Hey, sleepyhead," she said.

"I woke up to find you gone. No fair sneaking out."

"You looked so peaceful. I didn't have the heart to wake you. Besides, the doctor said you're supposed to get plenty of rest. I'm just making sure you follow his orders."

He stopped beside her, reaching up to trail the tips of his finger along the side of her neck to her ear. A shiver shot through her. One simple touch from his hand was enough to recreate all the feelings of want and need inside her. His touch was magical.

"I'm tired of napping."

He pulled her up and pressed her to his lean frame. Bending his head, he laid down a series of kisses where his finger had just stirred her passion, nibbling his way across to her mouth. Her mouth opened under his, sharing something wonderfully sweet and delicious. Something familiar but equally new.

He lifted his head to stare down into her eyes. His smile, slightly crooked, held a teasing quality to it, a smile that melted her insides to the consistency of sun-warmed honey. "I can think of a lot more interesting things to be doing in bed than napping."

She whipped off his cap and ran the flat of her hand over the short bristles of his hair. It was growing back nicely. Her fingers lightly traced the scar on the left side of his scalp. It was healing well, too. Soon his hair would cover it completely and there'd be no evidence it was even there.

He'd come through surgery to relieve the pressure on his brain with flying colors. But the thought that she could have lost him tied a hard knot in the pit of her stomach. She would have been lost without him.

"Getting a little frisky, aren't you, baldy? I'm not sure your neurosurgeon would approve."

"Who cares about him? He does nothing for me. Now, my live-in doc, that's another matter entirely. She drives me wild."

"Not a doctor yet," she corrected, giving him a playful shove with her hip.

"You will be soon. Your residency starts in less than three months." He slipped his arms around her, his hands slipping down over her hips and holding her snugly to him. "Decided yet if you're going to marry me and stop being a kept woman?"

She snorted. "Kept woman? I'm the one with the steady job, big guy. You've been laying around in bed far too long to consider yourself the breadwinner in this family." She replaced his cap, turning it a jaunty angle before standing on tiptoes to kiss him again. "But yes, I've made my decision. I'll marry you under one condition."

"What's that?"

"No more ice climbing—" she had to suppress a giggle at the look of horror that flickered across his face "—until your doctor gives you a clean bill of health."

"Good save, Doc. You almost lost a potential husband."

She laughed. "Don't worry. I get the fact that you're part mountain goat. Hopefully the kids will get my brains and innate cautious nature."

He laughed, loving her playfulness, the depths of her passions that he was only beginning to discover. Something told him that he was going to enjoy delving even deeper in the years to come.

She tilted her head back and met his gaze. "You know, you never told me what happened between you and Detective Denner when he stopped by your hospital room a week after surgery."

"Are you asking if he got down on his knees and begged my forgiveness?"

It was her turn to laugh. "Somehow I can't picture that."

"Good...because he didn't."

She raised an eyebrow. "No apology?"

"I can't say that. But what ever it was he offered that day, it wasn't what you'd call heartfelt. But I guess it was the best apology the guy could manage considering how he felt about me." Michael shrugged. "For some reason, I think he really wanted it to be me. Ticked him off royally that he had missed the mark so completely. He isn't the kind of guy who enjoys being wrong."

"Maybe if he hadn't been so sure it was you, he could have figured things out sooner."

A warm breeze swirled around them, lifting her hair and ruffling the collar of her shirt. He wrapped an arm around her and turned to leave. "He needed you to do that for him."

"Beginner's luck."

"No, not luck. Trust." He tucked a strand of hair behind her ears, his fingers trailing along her cheek. "Did I remember to thank you for believing in me?"

She nodded. "More times than I can count."

"I'm glad because I don't think anyone else, myself included, had anywhere near your level of trust in my innocence. It was a pretty amazing thing."

"Not when you have someone like you to trust in, Michael."

He tugged gently on her, urging her toward the trail back to the lodge. "Come on, I'm ready to head back to the city."

"Wait," she said, leaning down to pick up the tiny bunch of daisies lying on the rock.

"What are those for?"

"A present for Andrea. I promised Gracie the night she was taken into custody that I'd bring them up here this spring."

She paused and looked at Michael. "Do you think she's going to be okay?"

"Nikki and I have arranged for the best legal defense team there is."

"But she's never going to be really okay, is she?"

"I don't know. Nikki says that she isn't responding to anyone. She just sits and talks to Andrea. I think she's lost, buried under a sea of guilt."

Kylie nodded sadly and then stepped to the edge of the cliff. She threw the flowers out into the center of the gorge. They arched upward, petals and stems flashing pure white and brilliant green in the setting sun.

Slowly each one drifted down, settling on the crest of the current and disappearing beneath the spray.

"Safe journey, Andrea," she said softly before turning and walking away, leaving the memories of childhood where they belonged.

Finally ready to start her new life.

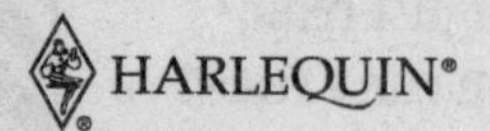

INTRIGUE®

COMING NEXT MONTH

#897 CRIME SCENE AT CARDWELL RANCH
by B.J. Daniels
Montana Mystique
Former lovers reunite to dig up their families' torrid pasts and reveal the secret behind the skeleton found in an old dry well.

#898 SEARCH AND SEIZURE by Julie Miller
The Precinct
Kansas City D.A. Dwight Powers is a street-savvy soldier in a suit and tie. His latest case: saving the life of a woman caught up in an illegal adoption ring.

#899 LULLABIES AND LIES by Mallory Kane
Ultimate Agents
Agent Griffin Stone is a man that doesn't believe in happily ever after. Will private eye Sunny Loveless be able to change his mind?

#900 STONEVIEW ESTATE by Leona Karr
Eclipse
A young detective investigates the murderous history of a hundred-year-old mansion and unearths love amidst its treacherous and deceitful guests.

#901 TARGETED by Lori L. Harris
The Blade Brothers of Cougar County
Profiler Alec Blade must delve into the secrets of his past if he is to save the woman of his future.

#902 ROGUE SOLDIER by Dana Marton
When Mike McNair's former flame is kidnapped, he goes AWOL to brave bears, wolves and gunrunners in the Alaskan arctic cold.

www.eHarlequin.com

HICNM0106